...er slammed her knee into the desk when she caught her first glimpse of Trevor's broad back, lean waist and tight behind

White-hot pain shot up from her knee and exploded into tiny stars in her head. She gripped the edge of the desk and bit down on her lip to keep from screaming.

But the real cause of the heat that flooded her cheeks and set her heart racing was when Trevor looked over his shoulder at the sound of the collision.

For a moment, she couldn't think beyond the pain in her knee and the vision before her. Trevor Jackson was not the stumpy, balding, cigar-chewing, dirty-under-the-fingernails contractor that she'd expected. He was an Idris Elba look-alike, with the build and piercing dark eyes to cinch the deal. If he opened his mouth and spouted the King's English, she was done. His right eyebrow lifted and she only wished her lashes were as naturally thick as his.

Concentrating on standing up without wobbling on her aching knee, she made it to her feet as he turned fully around. Her stomach fluttered.

"Mr...." Her mind went blank.

"Jackson."

Books by Donna Hill

Kimani Romance

Love Becomes Her
If I Were Your Woman
After Dark
Sex and Lies
Seduction and Lies
Temptation and Lies
Longing and Lies
Private Lessons
Spend My Life with You
Secret Attraction
Sultry Nights

DONNA HILL

began writing novels in 1990. Since that time, she has had more than forty titles published, which include full-length novels and novellas. Two of her novels and one novella were adapted for television. She has won numerous awards for her body of work. She is also the editor of five novels, two of which were nominated for awards. She easily moves from romance to erotica, horror, comedy and women's fiction. She was the first recipient of the *RT Book Reviews* Trailblazer Award, won an *RT Book Reviews* Career Achievement Award and currently teaches writing at the Frederick Douglass Creative Arts Center.

Donna lives in Brooklyn with her family. Visit her website, www.donnahill.com.

SULTRY *Nights*

DONNA HILL

KIMANI™ ROMANCE

This book is lovingly dedicated to all of my readers
who have continued to support my work for twenty-one years!
I could not have done it without you.

 KIMANI PRESS™

Recycling programs
for this product may
not exist in your area.

ISBN-13: 978-0-373-86252-8

SULTRY NIGHTS

Copyright © 2012 by Donna Hill

www.kimanipress.com

Printed in U.S.A.

Dear Reader,

I hope you are all excited to finally get your hands on the third book in my Lawsons of Louisiana series. You've already met the family, and each of them has a story to tell. This time, feisty Dominique takes center stage when she comes head-to-head with Trevor Jackson. Dominique is spoiled, rich and used to getting what she wants. Trevor couldn't care less, and that really ticks Dominique off. But things aren't what they seem at all.

When I originally started thinking about my next Lawson book, it was titled *Risky Business* because, as we all know, mixing business with pleasure is nothing but trouble. And Dominique and Trevor have more trouble than either of them bargain for. Fortunately Trevor has a good friend in Max Hunt (Ladies, he is fine! with a capital *F*), and he can offer sound advice. (I know readers are going to want a story about Max!) And thankfully Dominique has her sisters and her good girlfriend Zoe (from *Legacy of Love*) to share her angst.

Of course the rest of the Lawson clan, as well as their significant others, will be making an appearance. So you will have a chance to catch up on everyone. I know readers have been asking for Rafe's story. I'm saving him for me… I mean for later. So savor him while you can, because it's going to take a special woman to tie him down.

In the meantime, put your feet up, grab something cold and welcome to the steamy, sultry world of Dominique Lawson and Trevor Jackson.

Until next time,

Donna

Chapter 1

Dominique Lawson frowned as she fussed with her father, Branford's, bow tie. "Daddy, if you would stand still I can get it straight. What are all those guests going to say when they see the great Senior Senator Branford Lawson walking his daughter down the aisle with a crooked bow tie?" She adjusted the edges and smoothed the starched white collar of his tuxedo shirt.

"They're gonna say those Lawson girls must be costing ole Branford a fortune with all these weddings." He huffed in feigned annoyance and tugged on the lapels of his jacket. "First Lee Ann and now Desi."

"Well, Daddy, you don't have to worry about me. I won't be getting married anytime soon—if ever." She patted his broad chest with a delicate hand. Her Vera Wang bridesmaid gown in a shimmering honey-tone rustled ever so softly when she moved away.

"You say that now. But when the right man comes along, you'll be singing a different tune."

"Don't count on it. I love my freedom to come and go as I please. I love my independence as a business woman and I'm not ready to give that all up to kowtow to the whims of a man—especially on a regular basis." She pursed coral-tinted lips.

Branford tucked in his smile. It was true, of his three daughters Dominique was in a class all by herself. She and her twin sister, Desiree, couldn't be more different. Dominique was defiant against authority from the time she was in the crib. She was free-spirited and had more men sniffing at her heels than he would like. She enjoyed variety and her relationship attention span was like that of a five-year-old. He'd long ago lost count of whom she was seeing. And she spent money as if it grew on trees in the yard. It was a miracle that the non-profit organization she'd started hadn't gone under. He was sure it was his eldest daughter, Lee Ann's, wise but firm counsel that was the salvation for the business. Dominique was the female version of her older brother, Rafe, whom he'd all but given up on ever settling down.

"You two almost ready?" Lee Ann called out, poking her head in the bedroom door.

Whenever Branford looked at his daughter Lee Ann he saw the younger version of his beloved wife, Louisa, and his heart ached a bit at the memory. Lee Ann was delicate in a way that Louisa was not, but she had Louisa's facial structure and the very same light in her eyes. She also had the uncanny ability to manage her life and the Lawson clan without missing a beat.

"Well, don't you look 'matron of honorish,'" Dominique said with a grin. "Love the new hairdo," she added, acknowledging Lee Ann's short, tapered hairstyle.

"Not looking too bad yourself, little sis." Lee Ann came fully into the room and stood at the foot of the bed.

"Where's that husband of yours?" Branford asked, checking his diamond cuff links.

Lee Ann's face lit up from the inside at the mention of her husband, Preston. They'd been married less than a year and even with the hectic life of being a senator's wife and all that entailed, the glow of being newlyweds had yet to wear off.

"He's in the den talking music and football with Rafe and Justin and trying to stay out of everyone's way," she said laughing. "The decorators are finished. Downstairs looks like a wonderland. Oh, my goodness. And the yard is truly heaven. The caterers are setting up and the band should be here in about an hour. The guests are going to be blown away. Oh, the photographer is here, Dom. He wants to start getting some photos with us and Desi before we head over to the church."

Dominique patted her hair. "Always ready for my close-up." She hooked her arm through Lee Ann's.

"You okay, Daddy?" Lee Ann asked as the sisters started for the door.

"Of course, why wouldn't I be?"

Lee Ann eased away from Dominique and walked back to her father. "I know you're wishing Mama was here," she said softly. She tenderly touched his strong jaw. "But she is." She smiled, kissed his cheek then wiped the lipstick smudge with the pad of her thumb. "She would be very happy."

Branford swallowed over the sudden knot in his throat, then cleared it roughly. "You all better go on and see about your sister."

Lee Ann's eyes lovingly flickered over her father's face for a moment before she turned and joined Dominique.

Dominique tapped lightly on Desiree's bedroom door. "It's us," she called out and opened the door.

Desiree was seated at her dressing table and spun slowly around on the stool when her sisters entered. Joy radiated from her like the morning sun blooming across the horizon.

Dominique's hands went to her mouth, gasping in awe as she was struck by the vision that was her sister. She looked like a descended angel in the strapless ivory gown with its stitched bustier and tumbled layers of lace and organza that floated away from her small waist in a burst of diaphanous perfection. Her hair that she generally wore wild and free was pulled away from her face into a sleek bun that accentuated her sharp cheeks and wide eyes. A single white lily, reminiscent of Billie Holiday was tucked in her hair. Diamond studs that her mother, Louisa, and her sister Lee Ann had worn on their wedding days sparkled in her lobes.

"Oh, Desi," Dominique whispered, quickening her step into the room. She reached for her sister's hand. "You look…incredible." She could feel her eyes begin to tear up and she sniffed hard. She was not going to ruin her makeup. "Girl, you are absolutely beautiful," she said in an awed whisper. This was the woman who shared her same face but was as different from her as apples to oranges. Desiree's idea of being fashionable was a business suit, and when she wasn't in corporate mode she was behind the wheel of some race car in a grimy jumpsuit and a helmet. Dominique slowly shook her head. "Wait til Spence sees you. He's gonna run *up* the aisle to meet you!"

The sisters burst into laughter.

Lee Ann stepped up to her younger sister and tenderly braced her shoulders. "You are going to make a beautiful bride, an amazing wife and awesome mom… when the time comes," she added. "I'm so happy for you, sis."

"I can't believe I'm getting married," Desi said a bit breathlessly.

Their brother Justin knocked on the door and stuck his head in. "The photographer is getting anxious, ladies."

"Send him up, J," Lee Ann said.

"Looking good, baby bro," Desiree called out.

Justin, the youngest of the Lawson brood, had truly grown into his looks, bypassing his older brother, Rafe, by an inch in height with a body that had filled out and become defined and sculpted from his weekly workout. Justin's smooth mint-chocolate complexion made women want to run their hands across his face and check if those deep dimples were real. As much as he could have been a serious Louisiana playboy, Justin was totally focused on his education and following in the footsteps of his father.

Justin winked at his sister in response to her compliment. "I'll send him up," he said before shutting the door.

The sister's did last-minute makeup and hair checks before the photographer arrived.

"Dom, have you settled on a contractor yet for the expansion of First Impressions?" Lee Ann asked as she added a hint more lipstick and straightened the diamond necklace that Preston had given her on their wedding day.

"The cutoff for bidding was last week Monday. I have to review all the submissions to see where I'll get the best deal."

"Don't wait too long. With the new tax incentive initiatives for small businesses to hire and the infrastructure push across the country, good contractors will be getting scarce."

Dominique adjusted the top of her dress. "Can you imagine that there might be a shortage of workers when for the past couple of years they had no jobs at all? The tides have finally started to change."

"And not a minute too soon," Lee Ann added.

"Okay, enough talk about business. Today is my wedding day. The only conversations should be what I'm going to wear—or not wear—on my honeymoon!"

They all laughed and slapped palms just as the photographer knocked on the door and the most important day in Desiree Lawson's life was in full swing.

The realization that she was going to lose another

sister was not lost on Dominique, no matter how much she tried to pretend otherwise.

Every photographer in the state of Louisiana must have been camped out on the steps and the streets bordering Shiloh Missionary Baptist Church, hoping to get that money shot of the bride and groom and, of course, the political and entertainment figures that made up the Who's Who guest list.

The forty-five minute service brought tears to the eyes of the most cynical of hearts when Desiree and Spence shared their personally written vows and professed their love for each other with God and four-hundred-plus guests as witnesses.

Yet, even with that many people on the guest list, the wedding planner and her team were miraculously able to make the reception feel intimate and personal from the seating arrangements to the decor.

The band played everything from zydeco to slow jams, R&B classics, to blues and jazz. Rafe joined the band and did a solo performance on his sax playing his rendition of "Just the Two of Us," by Grover Washington, Jr. in tribute to his sister and new brother-in-law.

Dominique did what she did best, flit like a bee from one flower to the next, teasing, cajoling and mesmerizing. But even as she remained one of the bright lights of the lavish affair she couldn't shake off a feeling of disconnect.

Everywhere that she looked, couples were laughing, hugging, kissing or looking for a corner to sneak away to. They all seemed to have someone to go home with, spend tomorrow and the day after with.

She reached for a glass of champagne from the tray of a passing waiter and took a short sip as her toffee-colored eyes moved around the room. Paul LeMont, her date for the evening, came up alongside her and placed a light kiss on her exposed neck. She didn't feel a thing, not a tingle, not a spark, even as the warmth of his lush mouth played against the fine veins of her throat and his whispered words hinted at what he had in store for her later. She would let him take her to his home tonight. Tonight of all nights she didn't want to sleep alone. And sleep is all they would do.

Dominique turned into his embrace and looked up at his cover model face. "Let's dance."

Chapter 2

Dominique navigated her Mercedes coupe in the direction of her office, turning onto Magnolia Court North before making the left onto Main Street into the heart of downtown Baton Rouge.

"It was so good seeing you and Jackson and the kids at the wedding," Dominique said, speaking into her headset to her best girlfriend, Zoe Beaumont-Treme. "I wish Cynthia could have made it."

"Me, too, but she was with us in spirit from Paris. Your aunt Jacqueline looked incredible. I haven't seen her in years."

"I know. Neither have we. She writes to Rafe every now and then from wherever she may be with her job. But her and dad haven't spoken since...Uncle David."

"That's really such a shame. When all else fails what you have left is family."

"She said she may stay in Louisiana for a little while before she picks up her next assignment. Who knows maybe she and dad will find a way to work through things."

"I hope so. Not to change the subject but I'm still wowing over your sister's dress. Is she back from her honeymoon yet?"

"They came home last week. She looks fantastic. I still can't believe Desi is married. She's now Desiree Hampton."

"Is Desi going to hyphenate her name?" Zoe asked.

"I don't know. Why is it that women have to take the man's name, anyway? It is so yesterday. Things are changing but not fast enough and until they do, I intend to hold on to my own." Not that she had any immediate prospects in that regard, but that was beside the point. It was the principle.

"Girl, when the right man comes along I want to be a fly on the wall to hear what you have to say then."

Dominique heard one of Zoe's twins crying in the background. "I hear duty calling."

Zoe laughed lightly. "Those are 'we're hungry cries.' I'd better go. I'll call you over the weekend. Maybe we can meet up for lunch."

"Sure. Take care. Kiss the kids…and Jackson."

"Will do. Bye, sweetie."

Dominique heard the call disconnect in her ear. An odd feeling of sadness swept through her. She and Zoe and Cynthia had been friends since they were little girls. When Zoe moved to Atlanta a few years earlier to pursue her career as a curator at the High Museum, and

Cynthia a year later to open her business, it was difficult but they still managed to get together. They took vacations, shared secrets and shoes, and then Jackson Treme stepped into Zoe's life and everything changed for good. Now she was a married woman with two-year-old twins. But at least she and Jackson had moved back to Louisiana, so they did get to see each other more often, and Cynthia had been thinking of expanding her business and opening a secondary location back in her hometown of Louisiana. It would be great to have her girls back again.

Dominique pulled onto her street and drove around the corner to the small lot behind her building and parked her car, cut the engine, dropped her cell phone into her purse and got out. The alarm chirped as she pushed through the doors of the back entrance.

Getting First Impressions off the ground was Dominique's pride and joy. Everyone in her very ambitious family—save for her older brother, Rafe—was involved in something important. Sure, she could have spent her days shopping and lunching and traveling, but with her best friends married or moved away she found her days becoming empty and meaningless. She wanted her father to be proud of her, too, and that would have never happen if she'd continued living her life the way she'd been living it. He'd threatened on more than one occasion to cut off her endless funds if she didn't get her life together.

It was her older sister, Lee Ann, who had helped her to explore some of the ideas that had been running around in her head. If there was anything that Dominique was good at it was shopping and clothes. Her first thought was to open an exclusive boutique and use her many contacts to supply one-of-a-kind items.

"That's wonderful," Lee Ann had said, "but who needs another exclusive boutique? Who is that helping? What about supplying quality clothing for women who can't afford them?"

That was the seed of the idea that materialized into First Impressions. It was a top-of-the-line clothing establishment that provided clothing to low-income women that were returning to the workplace or needed that special one-of-a-kind outfit for an event. It started off small, but after less than six months in business she could barely keep up. She had a full staff that screened all of the applicants, stocked the racks and kept up with inventory.

Dominique's sense of style and understanding of what each woman needed to make them feel special was an integral part of the company's success. Now, with a bit more than two years in business, she was ready to expand and include a training program for women as part of her services. To do that she needed more space.

For the past month she'd been reviewing applications from contractors and had finally narrowed down her search to one: T. Jackson Contracting. She'd heard great things about the company, and was impressed with their proposal. She had a meeting scheduled with the owner in less than an hour.

Trevor Jackson maneuvered his Range Rover down the narrow street, slowing periodically to search for the address. He stopped in front of the building with the teal-blue awning and plate-glass window. "First Impressions" was emblazoned in bright white letters. He turned the corner and found a parking space. He draped the strap of his camera around his neck, took his iPad to take notes and walked back to the entrance.

He opened the glass-and-wood front door and a bell chimed. From the outside the size was deceiving. It was much larger than he expected and everywhere that he looked there were racks and shelves of women's clothing, shoes, purses and accessories in glass cases.

"May I help you?"

He turned toward the sound of the voice. A good-looking middle-aged woman in a crisp navy-blue suit and pale pink blouse approached him.

"Hi, I'm looking for Ms. Lawson. We have an appointment."

"You must be Mr. Jackson."

"Yes."

She smiled. "I'm Phyllis. Dominique is expecting you. Let me show you to her office."

They walked around the racks of clothing to the back of the showroom and then down a narrow hallway. The walls were lined with framed photographs of women in a variety of settings and outfits.

"Those are pictures of our ladies," Phyllis said by way of explanation. "Most of them are single mothers getting back to work, or women who had been incarcerated and are starting life over again. Some are high school seniors that needed a prom dress. I was one of them," she added.

Trevor didn't try to guess which category she fell into.

Phyllis stopped and knocked on a closed door.

He faintly heard a voice from the other side say to come in.

Phyllis turned the knob and opened the door. "Mr. Jackson is here."

"Thanks, Phyllis," Dominique said from behind the frame of her computer screen. "Make yourself comfortable, Mr. Jackson," she said and continued typing. "I'll be right with you."

Phyllis eased out and Trevor stepped inside. He took a quick survey of the small, totally feminine office and crossed the room to view the framed photographs on a chrome wall unit.

He'd seen pictures of the Lawson family in the newspapers and on television for years that spotlighted the high-class parties, the politics, the weddings and even the scandals that swirled around the oldest son. He'd had some doubts about bidding on the job. He'd had his share of rich folk and their "issues," their demands and fickleness. It was his business partner, Max Hunt, who finally convinced him that it was worth doing. The work that the organization did—according to its brochure—fit into Trevor and Max's sense of service to the community. Although he preferred to work in low-income neighborhoods and help the families in the 9th Ward rebuild, this would be his one corporate project for the year.

Dominique swerved her chair from in front of her computer screen and slammed her knee into the desk when she caught her first glimpse of Trevor's broad back, lean waist and tight behind. White-hot pain shot up from her knee and exploded into tiny stars in her head. She gripped the edge of the desk and bit down on her lip to keep from screaming.

But the real cause of the heat that flooded her cheeks and set her heart racing was when Trevor looked over his shoulder at the sound of the collision.

For a moment, she couldn't think beyond the pain in her knee and the vision before her. Trevor Jackson was not the stumpy, balding, cigar-chewing, dirty-under-the-fingernails contractor that she'd expected. He was an Idris Elba look-alike, with the build and piercing dark eyes to cinch the deal. If he opened his mouth and out spouted the King's English, she was done. His right eyebrow lifted and she only wished her lashes were as naturally thick as his.

Concentrating on standing up without wobbling on her aching knee, she made it to her feet as he turned fully around. Her stomach fluttered.

"Mr...." Her mind went blank.

"Jackson."

She forced a smile and wondered if she looked as suddenly unnerved as she felt. "Yes, sorry. Mr. Jackson. I've seen so many people this morning."

Trevor let the comment go. Maybe she got a very early start, seeing that it was barely after nine. Either that or she was no different from the rest of the elite that he'd dealt with in the past who didn't care enough to know the names of the people that they employ.

Dominique's knee was pulsing in time to the thudding in her chest. She finally had the presence of mind to extend her hand in his direction. And what did she do that for?

Trevor's large work-roughened hand enveloped hers. His long fingers wrapped around her palm and gently squeezed.

Heat sluiced through her veins, filled her body, loosened her inner thighs and made her tiny pearl stiffen and twitch.

He was a full head above her, even in her heels, and she was forced to look up at him to make contact with eyes that were framed with thick lashes and orbs that were inky black, almost bottomless. There was a slight squint to his gaze as if he was staring into sunshine.

"Is it okay if I sit down?"

Damn, was she staring? Only the flickering light of good home training kept her from snatching her hand away. "Of course." She smiled and extended her scorched hand in the direction of the couch and briefly shut her eyes the instant he turned his back and willed herself to get it together—and grabbed the folder with his paperwork.

He would never know how stiff her knee was becoming the way she managed to catwalk across the short space to join him in the cozy seating area. She opted for the club chair and slowly eased down into the plush comfort of the seat. Her knee was on fire.

Trevor leaned back against the plump cushions and draped his arm across the back of the couch. The rolled up sleeves of his tan chambray shirt revealed the tight tendons of his arms and he looked quite comfortable, as if sitting in her office relaxed and nonplussed was something he did regularly.

Dominique ran her tongue across her dry bottom lip and then opened the folder that was on her lap. "So..." She glanced across at him and forgot what she was going to say.

"Yes?" The corner of his mouth flicked.

Dominique adjusted herself in her chair and switched her focus to the papers in front of her. "Well, as you know, my organization has plans to expand. We recently purchased the two floors above us and I need them converted into work space, well classrooms, a library and a resource center."

"Right."

He wasn't going to make this easy. "I've received dozens of proposals but yours met all of our criteria."

He nodded.

Dominique swallowed. "If you're still interested, we can discuss terms and when the work can get started."

"I'd like to see the space."

"Of course." She started to stand and winced at the pain in her knee. She gripped the side of the chair.

Trevor was halfway to her side. "You okay?" He almost grabbed her but caught himself.

She bobbed her head. "Fine." She pushed herself to a standing position. "I'll show you the space." She led the way out of her office, toward the back of the building and around to the side entrance that led to the upper floors.

Dominique gripped the wobbly wooden banister and

gritted her teeth as she mounted the stairs. She was going to need some ice and not just for her aching knee.

Trevor dutifully followed Dominique up the stairs, trying to keep his mind on the steps and not the gentle sway of Dominique's hips or the curve of her legs or the soft scent that she trailed in her wake. Fortunately, they wouldn't have too much contact. Once work began he couldn't imagine a woman like Dominique Lawson being in the mix of dust, buzz saws and sweaty men.

Chapter 3

Dominique opened the door onto the first floor that had once upon a time been an apartment.

"Here we are."

Trevor took in the space. The wood floors were warped and coming up in spots and some of the boards were missing. It was clear that there had been major water damage from the stains on the ceiling and the buckling walls. The kitchen would have to be ripped out completely along with the bathroom. The two back rooms that must have served as bedrooms were in no better shape. He took pictures as they walked through the space. Then they went up to the top floor that was in a similar state of disrepair before returning to Dominique's office.

Dominique stood in the center of her office and folded her arms in front of her. "So…what do you think?"

"Anything is doable. It will take some work but it can be done." He walked past her and caught another whiff of the scent she was wearing before sitting in the chair she'd been in earlier. He could almost feel her warmth.

Dominique perched on the edge of the couch with her delicate ankles crossed.

"I'll take a look at the pictures, talk it over with my partner and put some sketches together based on what you say you need. I can get back to you in about a week."

"A week…is great. How long do you think it will take to complete?"

"Once work is started, barring any surprises, about two to three months."

Her eyes widened. "Really? I had no idea it could be done so quickly."

He pushed up from his seat. Her gaze followed his rise.

"As I said, barring any obstacles." He gave her a half smile. He tucked his iPad under his arm and extended his free hand.

Dominique placed her hand in his. "I'll get the contracts drawn up as soon as I see the design," she said, sounding a little breathless even to her own ears.

"Fair enough."

"Can I offer you some coffee before you go?"

"Thanks. But no. I have another appointment."

She offered a tight smile. "I'll walk you out."

"I'm good. I'm sure you have things to do."

Inwardly she flinched. Was she being blown off?

She crossed the room to the door and opened it. "Thank you for coming, Mr. Jackson."

Trevor met her at the threshold. "I look forward to doing business with you, Ms. Lawson." He walked out, stopped then turned. "You really should get some ice on that knee."

The air got stuck in her throat. She didn't know if she was embarrassed or ticked off by his offhanded comment. It wasn't so much what he said, it was the delivery, as if he had one up on her.

She spun away from the door and her knee screamed. She slammed her office door shut, limped over to the couch and plopped down. For the first time she took a peek at her knee. It was already obviously swollen. Tenderly she placed her hand, the hand that was still warm from holding his, over the knee that throbbed beneath her touch.

Trevor's half grin and probing eyes seemed to tease her as she replayed their meeting behind her closed lids. There was nothing special about Trevor Jackson. She'd been with much more handsome men, men with money, class and prestige, men who would do just about anything to be with her. So, what was it about Trevor that had gotten so quickly under her skin?

He's just not that into you.

Her eyes fluttered open. Hmm. Not on her watch.

Why he drove around in pretty much a circle for nearly twenty minutes, he would never tell anyone. He couldn't get her scent out of his head or the way she ran her tongue across her lips. He considered himself well educated, comfortable in any situation and articulate. But for the life of him he'd barely been able to string a full sentence together.

Finally, he wound his way back onto the right road leading out of town to his office in New Orleans. It was a miracle that he hadn't run over someone's cat.

He pulled into the angled parking space in front of the three-story brick building that housed his construction company. There are some things you know in life, and the one thing that he'd known since he watched his uncle Reggie, who was a carpenter by trade, hammer a nail, was that he wanted to build things. Once he was old enough he spent his summers as an apprentice on construction sites, learning the trade, working, sweating, getting his hands dirty and loving every minute of it. But as his uncle had told him over and over, having brawn wasn't enough. He needed brains to go with it. So he went to school, got a BS degree in Construction Management and an MBA in Economics, both from Louisiana State University. Within two years of getting his construction management degree, he worked out a business plan, presented it to the bank and landed a small business loan that launched his first storefront office. At the time he was his lone employee, other than when he needed an extra set of hands, until Max came on board and signed on as a partner. That was nearly ten years ago. He was twenty-five and still wet behind the ears. Now he had a permanent staff of fifteen artisans, and subcontracts with dozens of other tradesman. He had one of the most successful privately owned construction companies in the state. He had more work than he could handle, but the one job he never turned away was his community service work, his way of giving back. Otherwise, he and Ms. Dominique Lawson would have never crossed paths.

Max Hunt was stepping out of his office door with a handful of blueprints when Trevor came in.

Max and Trevor had been best friends since grammar school. They liked the same things, sports, fishing, good music, hard work, a stiff drink and beautiful women. They'd been dubbed the Black Knights back in college, a reputation they seemed to have maintained into full manhood, matching each other stride for stride in the looks and sexual charm department except that Max resembled the clean-shaven Shamar Moore.

Max briefly glanced up then returned his attention to the blueprints. "Hey, man, how'd it go?" he asked, walking to the industrial copy machine.

Trevor took the camera from around his neck. "Pretty good."

Max lifted the cover of the copy machine and placed the blueprints facedown. The machine hummed and began spitting out copies. Max frowned and turned his head in Trevor's direction. "Pretty good. That's it?"

Trevor shrugged slightly and took the memory card out of the camera. "Took a tour, she told me what she needed. Said we got the contract. I told her I'd get back to her in about a week with some design ideas." He shrugged again. "That's it. Nothing to tell."

Max gave him a sidelong glance. "Yeah, right, my brother. What really happened?" He half smiled.

"What are you talking about? That's it."

"What did she look like in person?"

Trevor's eyes flashed for a moment but he couldn't stop the smile that slowly moved across his mouth. "Edible."

Chapter 4

Dominique spent the rest of the morning with her leg propped up on a short step stool beneath her desk with a plastic bag of ice on her knee, while she read over the latest inventory reports. Although her family, her father and oldest sister, Lee Ann, in particular, used to ride her relentlessly for her insatiable desire to shop, it was an obsession that was paying off with style in her business. All those days of racking up the charges in boutiques across Louisiana, and as far away as Milan and Paris, and cooing the sales reps, shop owners and up-and-coming designers, Dominique had, unbeknown to her, been building a foundation. Now it was all paying off in major ways. Her contacts were more than happy to accommodate her with their overstock, sample items and huge discounts for her non-profit organization.

The women who came to First Impressions with their

heads down walked out turning heads. And now she was ready to take her business to the next level and offer an education component that would include GED classes, financial management courses and interview preparation.

She turned to her computer screen and brought up the spreadsheet that included the staffing that she would need, along with the list of vendors that would supply the materials for the courses. If Trevor Jackson was on target with his completion date she would have to begin interviewing for instructors sooner rather than later.

Trevor Jackson. She leaned back in her seat. For the past hour she'd done well in casting him to the back of her thoughts. But much like a thunderstorm that was on the horizon, as much as you wanted to, you couldn't ignore it. You knew it was coming.

"How's your knee feeling?"

Dominique glanced up at her assistant, Phyllis. She smiled wanly. "Better thanks." She lifted the ice pack off of her knee and noticed that the swelling was all gone. Gingerly she lowered her leg from the step stool. "How's everything up front?"

"Good. The five new referrals will be here shortly."

Dominique checked her watch. It was nearly one. "Great. Let's order lunch and we can set up in the conference room."

"Anything in particular?"

"How about some wraps and salad?"

"I'll put in the order." Phyllis paused for a moment. "So, how did the meeting go?"

Dominique glanced up for a moment then looked

away. "Pretty good. I plan on giving him the contract. Mr. Jackson is going to work on some designs and get them to me next week."

Phyllis nodded slowly, noting that the very direct Dominique barely looked her in the eye. "So, you think he's the one?"

Dominique's head snapped up as if she'd been caught stealing. "Huh?"

"I mean do you feel he's the right person for the job?"

Dominique swallowed. "Yes. Why? Is there something that you know that I don't?"

"Hmm, nope." She tugged lightly on the hem of her suit jacket. "I'll go put in the lunch order." She turned away to hide her smile.

"Phyllis, wait."

Phyllis stopped at the door. "Hmm."

"You're always so good at first impressions—no pun intended—what…do you think of him?"

Phyllis folded her arms beneath her ample breasts. "I think if his work is half as good as his looks, the addition will be a real showstopper."

Dominique chuckled. "That's the best answer you could come up with?"

"First impressions, right? Well, that honey was my first impression. The rest is up to you." She gave Dominique a wink and walked out.

Dominique leaned back in her seat, tugging on her bottom lip with her teeth. Phyllis had been straight with her from the day they first met when she'd come to First Impressions needing a dress to attend her daughter's graduation. Even though she was in need, there was an assurance and a dignity about her that made Dominique feel that Phyllis was the one doing something for her and not the other way around. She reminded Dominique of her mother with her directness, warmth, plain words of wisdom and her ability to make everyone feel special.

They'd hit it off that very first day and while they talked and searched for the perfect dress, Phyllis subtly organized shelves and lined up the clothes on the racks as she moved through the space, answered the phone when Dominique was with another client and even showed a few around the establishment while Dominique was discussing inventory with one of her vendors.

"Seems like you could use a little help around here when it gets busy," Phyllis had said while Dominique wrapped up her purchase.

Dominique tilted her head to the side. "Are you busy?"

"As a matter of fact I have nothing but free time on my hands. I'd be more than happy to come in a couple of hours a day—just to help out," she'd added.

The couple of hours had turned into full days in no time, and quicker than that Phyllis had become Dominique's right-hand assistant. She came to depend on her for more than help with running the business. Phyllis had begun to halfway fill the shoes that the loss of her mother had left empty.

Which was why Dominique was perplexed by Phyllis's vague response to her question. Phyllis may be a lot of things, but ambiguous was not one of them.

As much as she wanted to dwell on Trevor Jackson, she didn't have time. The women would be arriving shortly and she needed to be focused so that she could provide each lady with the attention that she deserved. But no matter how hard she tried to stay on point during the next two hours, images of Trevor kept popping up in front of her.

Trevor loaded the images from his camera onto the twenty-seven-inch iMac. He pointed out the major problems to Max and they both took notes. Trevor explained what it was that Dominique wanted and for the next few hours they worked on a series of sketches for the revised layout of the two floors.

"I want to give her at least two options for each floor," Trevor said. He raised his arms over his head, stretching out the tight muscles in his back.

"By the looks of the walls and the plumbing issues that you mentioned, the problem isn't going to be in the design but what we find behind the walls," Max said.

Trevor nodded. "Exactly." He closed the screen that showed the design plans and pulled up the file with their subcontractors. "We're going to need a lot of hands on this one."

"Shouldn't be a problem. The guys like working with us. At least they know when they come to T. Jackson Contracting its not going to be a one-day job."

"And this will definitely last a few months. I think we should get Ray for the plumbing and Joshua for the electric. They've done good work for us before and have solid teams."

"As soon as the plans are approved I'll start looking into supplies and getting the permits in order."

"Cool." Trevor pushed back from his seat.

"Don't think I forgot about your comment, my brother."

Trevor's thick right brow rose. "What comment?"

"You know damn well what comment… *Edible.* You really think I'm going to let that one slide?"

Trevor half smiled. "Just an observation, that's all."

"Man, I know you better than you know yourself. When was the last time some woman had you at a loss for words? You could barely put a sentence together when you got back."

It had been a while since a woman had lit a match inside of him. Five years to be exact and her name was Vallyn Williams. To this day, simply thinking about her knotted his stomach. Vallyn had burst into his life and took him on a roller-coaster ride that he'd never wanted to end. He should have known better. They came from two different worlds. She was the daughter of a judge and her mother sat on every board in the state of Louisiana. She grew up vacationing at Martha's Vineyard and the Hamptons. Her college graduation gift was a six-month trip across Europe.

"Trust me, it's nothing but an observation. End of story."

"Hmm, yeah, okay." He gathered up his notes. "Got any plans for later? I feel like hitting a club, listening to some music, checking out some ladies. You game?"

"I'm down. Say around nine?"

"Yeah, I have some stuff to take care of at the house.

I'll give you a call around nine and we can figure out where we wanna hang." He tucked his drawings under his arm and checked his watch. "I'm heading out. I want to check up on the crew over at the Jennings job."

"We should be ready to turn the house over to the family pretty soon."

"If everything is up to par, I figure by next week."

The Jennings family had been victims of Hurricane Katrina. For the past five years they'd been living in a trailer with their three kids. Those were the projects that Trevor was most proud of. Seeing the faces of the families whose homes he'd restored or built was worth every ounce of sweat.

"That's what I like to hear. Okay, you take care of that and I'm going to put some finishing touches on these design proposals then head out."

"See you later."

Trevor opened the design program and reviewed the tentative layout. He could almost see Dominique walking through the renovated space and the expression on her face when she saw the transformation. He shook his head. Thinking about a woman like Dominique Lawson in a role other than employer would bring him nothing but trouble. That was the one thing he was sure about.

Chapter 5

Dominique put her key in the door and was gripped with the feeling of regret. She probably should have moved out of the family home a long time ago. With both her sisters gone, her father in Washington most of the year, Rafe doing his own thing and Justin busy with school and work, she felt like a fish out of water rambling around in the big house. So, she could have not been more surprised when she walked into the kitchen and found both of her sisters seated at the island counter chatting like they'd done as teenagers.

"Oh, my goodness!" She dropped her bag on the table and ran to her sisters.

The trio kissed and hugged and giggled in delight.

"What are ya'll doing here?" She glanced from one to the other in amazement as they took seats around the counter.

"This is a big legislative week on Capital Hill. Preston is working almost twenty-four hours a day. I told him I was going home for the weekend and he nodded and waved," Lee Ann said, laughing. "I still don't think he realizes I'm gone."

"And what about you, *Mrs. Hampton?* You're still a newly, newlywed, girl. I'm surprised Spence let you out of the bed."

Desiree blushed and flashed a secret smile. "I know." She giggled. "Well, you know Spence is opening a third club in the D.C. area. He's meeting with contractors and visiting sites all weekend. And I wanted to see my sisters. I called Lee Ann and here we are."

Dominique felt tears well in her eyes. She'd had no idea how much she missed her sisters until this moment. She sniffed. "Then we have to make every minute count. No telling when we'll get a chance to hang out again."

"Exactly," Desiree agreed. "So, what's the plan? You're the party girl."

Dominique's eyes crinkled with mischief. "Ladies, my list is long and varied, so be prepared for anything. And put on your dancing shoes," she added, hopping up from her seat.

"Sounds like…a Dominique plan," Lee Ann teased.

"Just be ready by nine," Dominique warned, waving a finger at her sisters.

"You think I'll have time to get some racing in this weekend?" Desiree asked as they started off toward their rooms.

Dominique and Lee Ann groaned in response.

* * *

The sisters-only weekend didn't seem nearly long enough. But the trio had squeezed in as much time to-gether as they possible could. Friday night they drove into New Orleans and visited three clubs in the Quarter. Up with the sun the following morning, they headed for a full day of pampering at their favorite day spa, Body Envy, that came complete with facials, a full body massage, manicure and pedicure, and lunch with champagne spritzers. And what would a day be with-out shopping on the list?

By the time they returned to the Lawson mansion on Saturday, the sun had set, but they'd been coddled and primped and loaded down with shopping bags.

"I should have gotten that pair of gray suede boots," Dominique complained as she balanced her bags under one arm and propped on her raised knee while she stuck the key in the lock. "They would have gone perfectly with that jacket."

"Sis, you have enough shoes to outfit a foreign empire," Lee Ann teased as she struggled through the door with her own bags.

"Maybe a tiny empire," Dominique tossed back. "Not a big one."

"You *do* need another zip code for your shoes," Des-iree added, depositing her oversize bags near the foyer table.

Dominique turned to her twin. "I'm surprised that you needed more than a tote bag, Desi. Everything you bought was no more than a few colorful frilly strings tied together to *look* like an outfit." She shrugged out of her cropped leather jacket and hung it in the closet.

Desiree blushed and feigned embarrassment. "Can I help it if Spence only wants to see me in next to nothing when we close the bedroom door?"

"Girl, don't start," Lee Ann added. "I swear Preston has gotten worst since we've been married. He's totally into garters and those little demi bras now." She giggled. "I have an entire drawer full."

Lee Ann and Desiree laughed and chatted and laughed some more about the myths of married sex life, something that Dominique could in no way relate to. They oohed and ahhed about the feel of waking up each morning with someone you loved, being eager to see them at the end of the day and never worrying again about your "date" for a big event.

Dominique sat at the table and nodded and smiled in all the right places. For the first time in her life she felt like the outsider, the fifth wheel, the tagalong. When it came to the Lawson sisters she was always the center of attention, the diamond that sparkled the brightest. She was the party girl, the one that the men flocked to and fell over. She was the one with a suitors' list that was the Who's Who of Louisiana. She was never without a date or a man to warm her bed at night. But sitting there listening to her sisters made her life suddenly seem vapid and pointless. *Did you really need a man to make you complete?* She'd never believed that before and wasn't sure if she did now. Yet, as she listened to her sisters, two of the most free-thinking, independent women she knew, talk about the men in their lives, it was as if they had suddenly bloomed to life under the sun of their husbands' gazes.

Lee Ann and Desiree jumped at the sound of Dominique's palms slapping down on the table. "Enough, okay." She cut a look from one sister to the other. "I get it. You're both in love and can't stop talking about it." She pretended to gag.

Lee Ann leaned back in the swivel stool and folded her arms. "Is that jealousy I hear coming from Ms. 'nobody is going to tie me down?'" she asked, her right brow rising every so slightly.

Two pair of doe-brown eyes settled on Dominique. She made a face.

"Jealous! Humph. You have got to be kidding? Look, you know me, I have more than I can handle. So, let's not even go there," she added, waving her finger back and forth.

"Me thinks thou doest protest too much," Desiree said in a poor imitation from Shakespeare. She flashed a grin.

Dominique rolled her eyes.

"Mmm," her sisters harmonized in disagreement.

"When you finally get the one that hits that spot…" Desiree closed her eyes and slowly shook her head. Her body quivered just a little.

Desiree and Lee Ann giggled some more and regaled over Desiree's recent wedding and reception.

Dominique sat back, apart, letting her thoughts join the conversation but not her heart. So much had happened that day. She'd lost another sister to the magic of love and marriage, and her aunt Jacqueline, the woman whom she emulated, had thrown her a serious curve ball. As quiet as it was kept, the conversation had struck a nerve and she'd been unsettled ever since. The words still played havoc with her nonchalant attitude.

"So, Desi has finally gone and done it," Jacqueline Lawson said, easing alongside Dominique.

The night air was filled with the scent of jasmine, expensive perfumes and colognes, and the tantalizing aromas of the massive spread that had fed the four-hundred guests. The sun was settling down across the horizon. The final rays spilled like overturned cans of paint across the lawn, the white tents and twinkling lights, bathing all in a wash of gold and orange. Laughter bubbled like the champagne in Dominique's flute.

She inhaled a soft sigh. "That she has." She turned toward her aunt. Jacqueline Lawson epitomized everything that Dominique envisioned for herself—brains, beauty, class, style and a fierce sense of independence and individuality

"Anyone special in your life?" Jacqueline asked.

Dominique waved her hand as if to dismiss the question. "Oh, you know Aunt J, I'm not the settling down to one man kinda girl. It's fine for Desi and Lee Ann, and Zoe, too. But I'm going to be just like you when I grow up," she teased.

Jacqueline glanced away then. "I believed that fairy tale once upon a time." She took a sip from her flute. Her gaze seemed to see beyond the horizon.

"Fairy tale?" Dominique almost choked. "You sure you haven't had too much champagne, Auntie?" She

laughed. Jacqueline didn't. "You're serious aren't you?"

Jacqueline placed a delicate hand on Dominique's bare shoulder. "Let's simply say that I've been there and done that and doing it alone...is not all that it's cracked up to be." She looked directly at Dominique. "There will come a time in your life when having some- one that means something to you, and you to them, will be the only thing that matters. What the shame is—" she finished off her champagne and deposited the empty flute atop the tray of a passing waiter "—is discovering at that crucial point that no one is there but you."

Dominique frowned. It had been a lot of years since her aunt had set foot in the Lawson mansion. The rift between her and her brother, Branford, affected the whole family. But it didn't stop Dominique from idoliz- ing her aunt; that made what she said that much more unsettling.

"Aunt J, is there something you're not saying? Is there some other reason why you came back after all this time?"

Jacqueline patted Dominique's cheek. "Don't mind me, sugah. One glass too many has made me all silly and nostalgic." She flashed her famous smile and saun- tered away, but Dominique wasn't able to shake off the feeling that her aunt wasn't telling her everything.

"Earth to Dom. Earth to Dom," Lee Ann called out, waving her hand in front of Dominique's face.

Dominique blinked away the images and tucked the

conversation away, something she hadn't shared with her sisters. "Sorry. What were you two waxing poetic about again?"

Desiree hopped down from the stool. "All wasted energy Lee, trying to change this girl's mind." She stretched her arms high above her head. "I'm going to take a long hot bath and turn in. Early flight in the morning," she added, looking at Lee Ann.

Dominique stood between her sisters and wrapped her arms around them. "Now, if I tell you two something, I don't want either of you to blow it out of proportion." She glanced from one to the other. "I met someone."

Desiree and Lee Ann's eyes widened.

"You?" from Desiree. "But what else is new?"

"You mean another someone, right?" Lee Ann teased.

Dominique stepped out of the circle. "Laugh all you want." She folded her arms.

"A minute ago you were the poster girl for independence. Now you want us to believe that you found someone that's going to last beyond the thirty-day expiration date."

"Fine! Laugh." She snatched up her purse and was about to stomp away.

"Okay, okay, we're sorry," Dominique pleaded. "Don't be like that. We were just teasing."

Lee Ann took Dominique's hand. "So…who is it?"

Dominique tugged on her bottom lip with her teeth for a moment before blurting out, "Trevor Jackson."

Chapter 6

It had been more than a week since his meeting with Dominique Lawson. They hadn't spoken since that day at her office until the phone rang.

"T. Jackson Contracting."

"Good morning, this is Dominique Lawson. How are you Mr. Jackson?"

Hearing her voice was like a sudden shot of adrenaline that made him knock over his mug of coffee. Its contents splattered across the blueprint for a job that Max had just given him. Trevor blurted an expletive and jumped out of his seat.

"Excuse me?"

"Sorry. Not you." He looked around frantically for some paper towels or napkins. "I'm fine, thanks." He pulled open one of the drawers and grabbed a wad of napkins. He sopped up the mess the best he could while cradling the phone against his ear.

"Did I catch you at a bad time? I can call back. It sounds like you were in the middle of something."

"No, not at all. A minor mishap." He tossed the soggy napkins into the wastebasket.

"I have the contract ready for you to look over if you have the designs completed. Fair exchange?" She laughed lightly.

He looked at the mess he'd made and knew it would take him a few hours to redo the drawings. "Actually, they are. I was putting on the finishing touches." He lowered himself into his seat.

"That's good news. I'm tied up all day today but if you're free, let's meet for dinner. I can bring the contract. You can bring the designs. We can talk, relax…. We both have to eat right?"

"Tonight? Sure. That sounds fine. Do you have someplace in mind?"

"I was thinking of Blanche's Chateau on Montgomery and 9th. Do you know the place?"

Did he know the place? Who didn't know about the Chateau? The prices weren't listed on the menu. You needed a reservation weeks in advance just to be lucky enough to get a seat by the kitchen. Everyone who was anyone ate there at some time or another. It was someplace that was not on his frequently visited list. Truth was, he'd never set foot in the place. He supposed this was Dominique's way of reminding him of her name and money.

"Sure, I know where it is."

"Perfect. I'll call over and make sure that Charles gets us a good table."

You do that. His jaw clenched.

"Does eight o'clock work for you?

His temples pounded. "I'll see you then."

"Oh, if you get there before me just let them know you're meeting me. They'll take good care of you."

"I'm sure they will." He was biting down so hard that he was on the verge of cracking a tooth.

"See you at eight," she said, her voice full of cheer.

"Eight."

It took all he had not hurl the phone across the room. Instead, he pushed back so hard from the chair that it went slamming against the wall, rattling the framed company licenses that hung there.

"That uppity…" He ran his hand across his face then his head and started to pace the cramped space. "Who does she think she is, anyway? Am I supposed to be impressed…intimidated…embarrassed? This her way of showing me who's boss?"

"That bad that you're talking to yourself?"

Trevor's pacing hitched for a second when he saw Max in the doorway then resumed.

"What the hell happened in here?" His eyes widened in alarm. The wall plaques and certificates were askew. If he wasn't mistaken it looked like a small pool of light brown liquid had found a home at the foot of Trevor's desk. He focused on the top of the desk. "Is that my blueprint?" He hurried into the room and lifted the limp page from the desk. "Aw, man, you got to be kidding me."

"I'll take care of it," Trevor snapped.

"You got that right. How'd you manage this and what has you so pissed off, anyway?"

"Her."

"Come again."

"Her. Dominique Lawson."

"I would ask for some coffee to get my thoughts to catch up to yours but it's spilled all over my blueprint." The sarcasm wasn't lost on Trevor.

"I guess you're gonna have to verbally bring me up to speed. What does *she* have to do with your foul mood and *this* fiasco?"

Trevor heaved a deep breath. "I just got off the phone with her and you know what she did? She invited me to dinner at some snazzy restaurant." He went on to explain the phone conversation.

By the time Trevor was finished, the small snickers that Max had held in erupted into full-blown laughter.

"Man, you have got to be kidding me. A beautiful woman invites you to one of the most exclusive restaurants in the state of Louisiana and you're pissed off. What you need to be doing is getting your *one* suit out of the cleaners." He chuckled some more.

"I'm glad I can amuse you. It's my calling."

"Look, man, I'm sorry. But for real… What's the problem? You could probably buy and sell that place without blinking an eye."

"That's beside the point. She doesn't know that. She thinks I'm some dusty, working slob that needs a job."

"And whose fault is that?" Max looked him in the eye.

Trevor turned away.

"I know you have your reasons for remaining Mr. Anonymous, but don't get ticked when folks buy into the charade."

Trevor rubbed his chin. "I have more than one suit, you know."

"Really? You mean you bought one since college graduation?"

Trevor's features creased. A low chuckle rumbled in his chest. "Very funny. I should go like this," he said, and stretched out his arms to display his plaid work shirt, faded jeans and construction boots.

"Forget about the front door. You wouldn't get past the parking lot." He took the damp blueprint and draped it over the drafting table to dry. "Let's go for a ride."

"Where?"

"My tailor does amazing work. And he's fast. I can't have you going to the Chateau and ruining my rep."

"*Your* rep?"

"Yeah, it might get out that we're business partners. I go there at least once a month when I have a lovely lady that I want to impress. And the suites upstairs…"

"Suites?"

"Yes. About a half dozen. Damned hard to secure one, though if you do, trust me, it's well worth it."

"I take it you've "secured one" from time to time."

"Of course." He grinned.

"Why am I not surprised?"

Max Hunt was not only a savvy businessman and brilliant designer, but a connoisseur of all things expensive: clothes, cars, homes and women. He didn't have the same hang-ups that Trevor did about the millions that they had amassed over the years, much of which was due to Max's astute understanding of the financial markets and Trevor's keen sense of what was going to take off and what wasn't. Together they were a formidable team, and as opposite on most issues as day and night—clothing being one of them.

"Trust me, he'll hook you up and believe me, my brother—" he stepped up to him and straightened the collar of his un-ironed plaid shirt "—you could really use it."

Max adjusted his burgundy tie and fastened the single button on his metal-gray Armani suit jacket that Trevor guesstimated cost at least a thousand dollars.

"How much is this going to set me back, Max?"

"Price is not a factor when you're trying to impress a woman."

"Who said I was trying to impress a woman?"

Max grinned. "You didn't have to. It's all over my blueprint." He laughed. "Come on, let's go."

"Wait, let me get this straight," Zoe was saying as she bounced one twin on her thigh and bottle fed his sister in the stroller.

Dominique looked on in amazement. It was still hard for her to put "mommy" and Zoe Beaumont-Treme in the same picture, but here she was. Totally domesticated, like a lioness that was raised by humans. Dominique fully expected that one of these days Zoe was going to realize that she was supposed to run free in the wild and she'd show up on her doorstep with a suitcase and a plane ticket to the Caribbean, saying, "let's go." But when Dominique witnessed the expression of pure adoration in Zoe's eyes when she looked at her babies, Mikayla and Mikai, she wasn't so sure if that day would ever come.

"You told Lee Ann and Desi that you met someone and that *someone* is your contractor?" she asked in utter disbelief.

"Something like that. They don't know he's my contractor."

"I don't even want to know why." She wiped Mikayla's mouth with a soft cloth. "Yes, I do. Tell me." She stared at her friend.

Dominique leaned back and folded her arms in a petulant motion. "All they could talk about was their husbands, how good it was to be in love," she said, dragging the word out so that it sounded like a bad recording. "How happy I would be if I finally found someone. All damn weekend. I got sick of it so I blurted it out." She frowned.

"But why your contractor?"

"They don't know him for one thing."

Zoe tilted her head to the side. "I hear *another thing* hovering around."

She unfolded her arms, placed her palms flat down on Zoe's kitchen table and leaned forward. "If I tell you this you have to swear that you aren't going to get all silly or have an opinion or make a face or say anything."

"Why don't I just leave the room? Or you could put a bag over my head."

"Very funny."

Zoe glanced down at Mikai who'd fallen asleep in her arms and Mikayla had drifted off, as well. Zoe grinned. "Nothing like nap time. Let me put them down." She carried Makai across the room to the playpen and gently lowered him, and did the same for his sister in an adjacent playpen. She returned to her seat opposite Dominique.

"Okay, I'm listening."

Dominique sighed. She told Zoe all about that first meeting, how she felt and how she couldn't stop thinking about Trevor.

For a minute or two after Dominique bared her soul, Zoe was speechless. She actually believed that Dominique was genuinely interested in this man, that he'd awakened not just her libido but something in her soul. She understood all too well that feeling of breathlessness, the inability to think clearly, that rush like hurtling downward on a roller coaster. She felt that way every time she thought about her husband. But for Dominique, this was major.

"Wow," she finally managed.

"That's it, *wow?*"

Zoe shook her head lightly, making her locks shift softly around her face. "It's just that I've never heard you talk like that about someone—and mean it. But, Dom, you have three problems from the gate."

"What?"

"First of all this is a man you know nothing about. Two, he works for you—always a no-no. And three, you're lying to your sisters, scheming on landing this man and attempting to do it by overwhelming him with all your money and your name. So not cool."

Dominique puckered her lips. "That's more than three things."

"You know what I mean."

Dominique did have the wherewithal to look mildly contrite. She pushed out a breath. "Is it wrong that I want to show him a good time—even if it is a business meeting? I'd do it with anyone else."

Zoe gave her a withering look.

"Maybe not everyone… But I have had business meetings at expensive restaurants before."

"Not with a man you had your eye on and not at the Chateau. Admit it, Dom, you're trying to dazzle him. Don't. It will be a mistake. And he's going to be your employee. *Employee* is the operative word here." Zoe's eyes widened to emphasize her point.

Dominique crossed her legs at the knees and rocked her ankle-booted foot back and forth. "Fine. You're probably right."

She lightly chewed on her thumbnail, a clear indication to Zoe that Dominique hadn't given up but rather was mulling over a new plan.

Chapter 7

Trevor stood in front of the six-foot maple-framed mirror that rested against his bedroom wall like a piece of art. He had to admit, the fit of the midnight-blue Hugo Boss suit was on point. Max's tailor certainly knew his stuff, and although it was not made-to-order, the alterations were impeccable. He adjusted his skinny silk tie, grabbed his wallet and keys from the dresser and walked out of his loft apartment.

He'd lucked out when he'd stumbled across the building he now called home five years earlier. It was known to have been the dwelling of the legendary Madame Cherise who ran the most lucrative "ladies of the night" business in the state from the early 1900s until 1989 when she died. After her death, the ladies eventually drifted off and by the early 1990s the building was completely abandoned until Trevor drove past it one day and knew that it was going to be his new home.

It had taken nearly a year of red tape but finally the property was his. For the next three years he worked on renovating every inch of the two-story building. The lower floor was divided into three enormous rooms that contained a full kitchen, media room and lounge, and opened onto the lush backyard. The upper floor, however, was his domain. Towering floor to ceiling windows wrapped around the entire front. The refinished mahogany floors and beamed ceiling gleamed throughout. Stainless steel appliances, granite countertops, a large island that could seat six and a double oven comprised the dream kitchen. It opened onto the sprawling living area with its mounted flat-screen television, fireplace and state-of-the-art stereo system. He'd erected a dividing wall that zigzagged to the spa bathroom and then the master suite with a king-size bed at the centerpiece.

The exterior of the building with its worn facade and overgrown vines belied the stunning interior. And that's just the way Trevor wanted it. This was his sanctuary, his one guilty pleasure, and if he wanted to remain as much behind the scenes as possible, having his home shine like a beacon was not going to help his cause.

He went out back to the three-car garage tucked beneath a towering willow tree. He eyed the Range Rover, the Porsche Cayman and the Benz CL65. He opted for the Porsche. It had been a while since he'd taken "Shelly" for a spin. He smiled as he slid behind the wheel of the sleek black machine, turned it over and felt the powerful engine purr beneath him.

Every now and then it did feel kind of good to shed the day-to-day dust, sweat and grime and revel in what his hard work had afforded him. But his conscience always raged a battle. He knew what too much of a good thing could do to people. He'd seen it, experienced it, had been a victim of it. And he'd promised himself that no matter how successful he became he would never turn into one of "them." Dominique Lawson was beautiful, sexy and smart, and she represented everything that he struggled against. So, he'd put on the monkey suit, broke out the wheels and even shined his shoes. But only for tonight. Ms. Lawson needed to get a small taste of who she was dealing with.

Dominique hosted gala events for dignitaries. She'd wined and dined with men in politics, entertainment, business and education, and she'd never blinked an eye or had a moment of doubt or hesitation. Yet, tonight she'd changed her outfit four times. She'd had to reapply her makeup and put on an extra swipe of deodorant. She couldn't figure out if she should wear open-toe shoes or sling backs, and her hands were shaking so badly that she'd poked herself in the eye when she was putting on her mascara.

She peered closer in the mirror. The redness was hardly noticeable. She blinked and blinked again. Hopefully by the time she arrived—if she ever got out of the house—it would have cleared up.

She spun toward her bed with her hands on her hips.

She eyed the line of clothing that covered her pillow-top mattress. Drawing in a deep breath of decision she settled on the champagne sheath that she knew gently hugged her curves without being too suggestive. The two-inch-wide straps were classy and didn't have the slip factor of spaghetti straps. She chose a thin platinum chain with a teardrop diamond that hung a breath above her cleavage. Tiny diamond studs for her ears. Toes out *and* sling back shoes—she couldn't go wrong.

Dominique assessed herself from every angle. Each inch of her oozed understated style; from her perfectly casual coif to the subtly sexy dress to the soft scent that wafted around her and all with just the right about of bling. She smiled. Hopefully, Trevor would arrive before she did. She wanted to make an entrance that would leave him wanting *her* on his plate.

Trevor pulled up in front of the Chateau and a red-jacketed valet was at his door before he'd taken the key out of the ignition.

"Welcome to the Chateau," the young man said, taking the keys.

"Thank you," Trevor murmured, not all that comfortable turning his baby over to a stranger. He stood at the curb as the valet whisked Shelly away and the next car pulled up to take her place.

Coming to the Chateau had all the pomp and circumstance, and bells and whistles of walking the red carpet at a movie premier. The doorman nearly bowed before pulling open the heavy glass-and-chrome door.

If he thought the entrance was over the top, it had

nothing on the sprawling multi-level circular interior with private banquettes, tables for two-to-four and others for larger parties. Gentle music whispered in the background over the soft hum of modulated voices and tempered laughter. The dim lighting bathed the entire space in twilight—that moment before the world settles into evening. Footsteps were silenced by the thick red carpet and every member of the staff looked as if they'd stepped off the cover of a "models are us" magazine. This was so not his scene. Being out of his element was an understatement. He had the overwhelming urge to loosen his tie that was suddenly choking him.

"Good evening. And welcome to the Chateau, monsieur. Reservation?"

Trevor's head snapped ever so slightly toward the sensual voice. He focused on the woman standing in front of him who made him believe that there really was such a thing as a size zero.

"Yes, thank you. Reservation for Lawson. Dominique."

The woman's composed expression awakened as if by the sun. "Oh, yes, Ms. Lawson. She's already here. Please follow me and I'll get you seated right away."

What choice did he have but to follow the come-hither voice and catlike gait that led him to a glass elevator? They rode up one level. The door opened onto a lounge, dotted with overstuffed couches, velvet chaises, conversational seating, a bar that spanned one half of the space and a small, jazz combo that unobtrusively entertained.

Everything and everyone seemed to "twinkle,"

Trevor thought in a moment of barely contained hilarity. All this for some dinner.

They turned a short corner and there she was. For just an instant he thought he might have stopped breathing. Only for a second, that was all he would ever confess to, under duress, of course.

She was perched on a stool at the bar. Her legs were crossed at that tempting, perfect angle. She held a flute of something bubbly inches from her painted lips. The smooth lines of her dress hugged her round derriere and exposed the silky skin of her back. If it were not for the soft sheen of the dress to separate it from her buttery flesh she would appear stunningly naked.

Without warning her stomach fluttered and her heart kicked up a notch. She slowly turned her head and the air lodged in her chest, hanging there for an instant before exiting in a soft whoosh.

He was coming toward her and it was as if the rest of the room receded. Her peripheral vision was gone. All she could see was Trevor. The hell with *her* making an entrance. Watching him was worth conceding the upper hand. His slow pantherlike stride, the broad expanse of his chest encased in that very GQ suit, with the winter-white shirt set against the rich chocolate of his skin had her wet. She slowly uncrossed her legs. Her nipples grew erect and the sensation sent a mild shiver along her inner thighs, making her pearl harden and twitch. She did have the presence of mind to put her drink down on the bar before she did something stupid—like spill it all over herself to douse the heat between her legs.

Dominique's smile dazzled him and he would have lost his footing had he not come to a stop inches from her. Her scent possessed him. He knew he was there for a business dinner but all he wanted to do right then was see what she looked like beneath that dress and hear her call out his name all night long. How he wished he'd been able to "secure" a suite.

"Sorry, I'm late," he said.

"Not at all. I was early." Her eyes raked over his face. "Would you like a drink before we sit down?"

Maybe a drink would mellow him out. "Sounds good. Hennessy on the rocks."

She swiveled toward the bar and placed his order. He snatched a quick look at her behind.

Dominique turned back to him. "They'll bring it to our table."

He barely noticed that the diminutive waitress was still standing there. "If you'll follow me," she said.

Dominique and Trevor were led to a cozy banquette that looked out onto the nightlife below. He held out her chair and when her arm brushed against him he felt himself stir. He briefly shut his eyes, willing the surge away before sitting opposite her. He adjusted his tie.

"Great suit," she said.

He glanced across at her from beneath his lashes. "Thanks."

"Big difference from when we first met."

He leaned back a bit in the chair and stared at her, forgetting that she simply enchanted him and remembering instead who she was and why he was there. "In other words, I clean up well." He picked up his menu and made a show of studying it, not waiting for a response.

Dominique recoiled as if she'd been slapped. What had she said that warranted that kind of reaction? Her throat tightened. She was paying him a compliment. She knew a good suit when she saw one and what he was wearing cost him plenty. Probably his entire two-week salary. He was being sensitive for no good reason.

She huffed and pursed her lips. She randomly glanced over the menu when a waiter seemed to appear out of thin air at their table.

"Ms. Lawson. It's good to see you again. It's been a while."

Dominique brightened. "Frank. How are you?"

"Well. What can I get for you and the gentleman tonight? Your usual?"

She comes here so often that she has a "usual"? Trevor glowered behind the veil of his menu.

"You know me so well," she cooed. She turned her dazzle on Trevor and it beamed right through his menu. "You have *got* to try the shrimp gumbo soup." She closed her eyes in pure rapture and released a soft sigh, and in that instant Trevor totally forgot what he was so ticked off about.

He smiled, placed his menu on the table and then glanced up at Frank. "If the lady says I must have it then I guess I have to do what the lady says."

Frank gave a short nod of his head. "Right away." And poof, he was gone as silently as he'd arrived.

Dominique reached for her glass of champagne. "You won't regret it," she said before taking a tiny sip.

"Are you sure about that?"

His gaze bore through her like a hot prod and her hand shook every so slightly.

"I try to be certain about everything that I say before I say it." She set down her glass.

The corner of his mouth lifted by a centimeter. "You didn't give me the impression that you were a woman who relied on precision but rather lived for the moment, on instinct."

She tilted her head to the side. "Really?"

"Hmm. Yes, really." He reached for his drink—held it. "Am I wrong?"

"I wouldn't say wrong. I would say that I'm a combination of precision and spontaneity. I know what I want, and so when I see it I go after it."

"Is that with everything or just with fancy restaurants?" His eyes picked up the light from the flame of the candle and sparkled with merriment.

"The evening is still young, Mr. Jackson. There's no telling what I may want before it's over."

Dominique's radiant smile heated him from the inside out. He took a long swallow of his drink and that only intensified the warmth. *Down boy.* He shifted ever so slightly in his seat.

A white-jacketed waiter appeared and placed a bowl of gumbo in front of each of them then deftly refilled their water glasses before quietly moving away.

The aroma of the gumbo was almost heady. Dominique hummed in pleasure.

"Let me know what you think." She leaned slightly forward and dipped her spoon into the bowl, revealing the mysterious valley of her breasts.

Trevor forced himself to concentrate on the bowl in front of him. She was right. The gumbo was a slice of heaven.

"I have no words," he said, finally setting down his spoon.

Dominique smiled in triumph. "Told ya."

She leaned forward and Trevor trained his eyes on hers refusing to let them dip and take a peek no matter how much they begged.

"Truth is—" she lowered her voice "—this place is just an upscale joint for some down home Louisiana food." She waved a hand around. "All this is for show. But you can't beat the service, the ambiance or the chef!"

"So I see. And what would you recommend for a main course?"

She tossed her head back and laughed and he memorized the slender length of her neck. "That is a loaded question. But—" she raised a finger "—I would be remiss if I didn't insist that you order the stuffed crabs and dirty rice. I guarantee you will always be indebted to me." Her smile was a dare.

"You're on, Ms. Lawson."

Her right brow rose an inch. "After you taste the entrée I know you'll be calling me Dominique." She winked and finished off her glass of champagne.

The entrée arrived and Dominique was right. It nearly melted in his mouth it was so good. The music was mellow in the background, the atmosphere perfect and the vision in front of him left nothing to be desired.

They talked through dinner and Trevor had to work hard to contain himself while Dominique acted all upper crust and sophisticated while whispering to him all manner of gossip and rumor about nearly everyone in the place. She was wickedly hysterical. He'd heard her whisper "don't look now" so many times during the evening just before she'd launch into a raunchy story that he simply didn't bother to look beyond his plate, only into her eyes.

"Don't look now," she whispered, "but the woman in the red dress is one of the most notorious social climbers in Baton Rouge. She's been on the arm of every anybody."

"How am I ever supposed to know who you're talking about if I can never look?"

She brought the napkin to her mouth and giggled. "True. Okay, okay. You can look. Three o'clock by the window."

Trevor slowly turned his head toward the window and time came to a screeching standstill. The muscles in his neck tightened.

"Are you okay?"

Silence.

"Trevor. You okay?"

His head snapped in her direction. The red-hot heat moved from in front of his eyes and he could see clearly again. He cleared his throat, reached for the glass of water and took a long swallow. He set the glass down.

"Is something wrong?"

"No." He chuckled. "Sorry, guess I was daydreaming for a minute." He pushed back from his seat. "Going to the restroom."

Dominique followed his exit with her eyes and wondered what had gotten under his skin like that. She glanced across the room and watched as Vallyn Williams smiled up into the face of whom Dominique believed was the councilman for the 7th ward. She and Vallyn had crossed paths before at various events over the years. She'd never particularly cared for her for some reason. She shrugged.

Trevor took the hand towel from the attendant and wiped the water from his face. He stared at his reflection in the mirror. How long had it been since he'd seen Vallyn, one year, two? It would never be long enough. He straightened, adjusted his tie and returned to his table. He dared to look at where he'd last seen Vallyn but she was gone.

"Everything okay?"

Trevor sat down. "Fine."

Dominique studied him for a moment. Something had severed the hot wire between them. She knew when a man wanted her and it had been clear in every move, every look he'd made throughout the evening, that he did. Now there was a distance that hadn't been there before.

"We have yet to discuss the project," he said. He signaled for a passing waiter. "Another Hennessey, please."

Dominique dampened her lips with a slow swipe of her tongue. "Of course."

Trevor opened his iPhone and showed her the finished designs. She should have been studying the designs, but she was watching his long fingers as they swiped the screen to display a new image. The low rumble of his voice as he described the details of the layout was almost hypnotic. She was so hot she was sure she would implode. All she could think about was finding the right moment to invite him up to the suite.

"They're perfect."

The waiter came and cleared away their dishes. "Dessert?"

Dominique looked to Trevor.

"No. Thanks. You can bring the check."

Dominique reached across the table and covered his hand.

The shock of her touch curled his fingers. He looked into her eyes before drawing his hand away.

"I invited you. My treat."

His fingers curved into a fist. "I can take care of a dinner," he said in a hard whisper. His eyes bored into hers.

Dominique sat back. "Does my paying infringe on some macho sensibility?"

His jaw clenched. "It would take more than a dinner bill." He pushed back from the table and stood. "I think it may be best if you found someone else for your project."

Her mouth opened and closed.

"Good night, Ms. Lawson." He turned and walked out, just as the waiter returned with the bill.

Dominique held the leather folder in her hand and smiled.

Chapter 8

Trevor cut a new groove in the concrete while he waited for his car to be brought to him. Every muscle in his body was strung so tight that he knew the slightest nudge would make him snap. And that's when he looked up and saw Vallyn staring at him.

She was on the arm of the man from the restaurant. For a moment he thought she was coming toward him. But their car pulled up. She walked around to the passenger side. The valet opened the door and she got in. And then they were gone.

"Your car, sir?"

Trevor readjusted his focus and mindlessly took out his wallet, paid a tip, got in his car and drove off. He drove around for an hour or more with no specific destination in mind until he found himself by the piers. He parked and got out.

The night was still warm, clinging almost, but the soft breeze off the Mississippi kept the evening from being stifling.

He strolled along the dock until he reached a row of benches. He sat, stretched out his long legs, draped his arm along the back and looked off at the horizon. Laughter floated toward him and he saw a couple walking along the dock, all but inside each other's clothing they were so close.

He'd been happy like that once. At least he thought he was happy. When he met Vallyn Williams he was just getting his business off the ground. It was rough back then. Katrina hadn't hit yet and contracting jobs weren't steady. But he'd managed to secure a renovation contract with Cal Williams, the head of Williams and Masterson, one of Louisiana's high-end law firms. They handled major litigation for Fortune 500 companies. Williams was worth plenty. So, when Trevor got a call from Mrs. Williams to do a renovation on their guesthouse he couldn't have been more surprised. The job took three months to complete. It was during that time that he'd met Vallyn. They couldn't have been more different. Yet she always seemed to find a reason to stop by the work site to chat or ask questions that began to evolve from the details of the work to what movies and music he liked to his favorite foods. The day the job ended and he was packing up, Vallyn invited him to a party—casual she'd said. Feel free to bring a friend, she'd added. She gave him the address. He brought Max, who fit in like a foot in a shoe. Trevor, on the other hand, stood out like a pimple on a Cover

Girl commercial. However, Vallyn didn't give him too much time to feel out of place. That was the first night. There were more than he could count after that and then one day—

The boom of the ship's horn shook him out of his trip down memory lane. He glanced around, pushed himself up from the bench and walked back to his car.

"You did what?"

"Told her to get someone else for the job."

Max ran a frustrated hand across his head while he paced in disbelief. "I don't get it. Because she offered to pay for dinner?" he asked, his voice rising with incredulity. "You know how many men *wish* a woman like that would foot that kind of bill? Man, are you out of your mind or what?" He paused a moment. "Or was it seeing Vallyn out of the blue?"

"That's not the point."

"Then enlighten me, my brother. What is the point?"

"Forget it, Max. We don't need the job. We sure don't need the money." He spread out a set of drawings on his drafting table.

Max looked at his friend with a mixture of frustration and wonder. "And it's a lucky damned thing that we don't." He pointed a finger at Trevor. "She got to you. That's the real deal and it doesn't have anything to do with paying a bill." He shook his head and strode off to his adjoining office.

Trevor shoved the prints off his desk and watched them flutter to the floor. He would have preferred if something crashed instead.

* * *

Dominique had barely slept. She'd had it all figured out. She would wine and dine and tease him a little and then invite him up to the suite that she'd reserved so that they could discuss the terms of the contract in private.

She hadn't planned to spend the night alone. But her little plan backfired—big-time. Grudgingly she had to admire the fact that he could actually walk away from a lucrative job offer and her. After she'd gotten over the shock, she'd realized that Trevor Jackson's dismissal of her was a turn-on. She'd never had a man stand up to her before. And she'd never gone after something or someone that she didn't get. It was a brand-new feeling.

All night she'd vacillated between being pissed off and determined. By daybreak determined had won out.

Her GPS announced that she had arrived at her destination. For a few moments she sat in the car going over in her head what she was going to say. She drew in a long breath, stepped out of her car and walked up to the entrance.

It was a nondescript building. Pretty much what she'd expected. She pulled open the wooden door and stepped inside. The exterior was deceiving. She thought it would be more of a storefront setup—small and dusty. But it was cavernous. There were workbenches and scary-looking equipment. There was an unmanned desk up front and several workmen walking around, carrying lumber and tools. She walked farther inside and noticed that the space led all the way to the back but there appeared to be several rooms off to the side. She stopped one of the workmen.

"Excuse me, I'm looking for Trevor Jackson."

The man adjusted his hard hat. "Second door on the right." He hooked a finger over his shoulder.

"Thank you." She could hear saws buzzing in the background.

"Watch your step," he called out.

Dominique gingerly walked around tables and stacks of lumber until she reached the second door. It was closed. She squeezed her eyes shut for a moment, ran over what she was going to say and then she knocked.

"Yeah…come in."

She turned the knob and slowly opened the door. When Trevor glanced up from his worktable everything that she'd committed to memory went completely out of her head. She felt warm all over and her heart was suddenly racing so quickly that it was hard to breathe.

His mechanical pen tumbled to the floor. Slowly he stood up.

They both spoke at once.

Trevor held up his hand. "Okay, I give up. You first. What are you doing here?"

She held the leather folder with the contracts against her chest. "I came to apologize."

His brows drew together. "For what?"

"For whatever I did that offended you."

He studied her for a moment. She was simply beautiful. And at that moment, with her looking vulnerable and soft, all he wanted to do was take her in his arms and swear to her that whatever was wrong in her world he would make it right.

"I wasn't offended," he lied.

She angled her head slightly to the side. "Then what was it?"

He looked away for a moment then back at her. How could he explain his personal pet peeve to her? He came from behind the desk.

"Have a seat, Ms. Lawson."

Dominique crossed the space to an empty chair and sat. Trevor pulled the chair from behind the table and straddled it. He rested his arms across the backrest. "Look, I probably overreacted."

She arched a pretty brow. "You think?" she said in a teasing tone that elicited a smile from him.

"I'm my own man, Ms. Lawson. And I won't put myself in a position to be perceived otherwise."

She languidly crossed her legs and Trevor's breath hitched in his chest.

"Understood," she said, although she really didn't.

The hot air hung between them.

Dominique stood. "Can we start over?" She walked over to him and extended her hand. "My name is Dominique Lawson and I'd like to hire you to do some major renovations."

Trevor's dark eyes danced across her face. Slowly he stood up and took her hand. His long fingers enveloped hers. "Trevor Jackson. I have some designs I think you'll like."

Dominique's smile bathed him. "I'm sure I will."

* * *

They talked for more than an hour, going over the specifics of the designs for each of the rooms, making a few changes along the way and going over the terms of the contract.

Trevor had to admit that he admired Dominique's inquisitiveness, her ability to understand the mechanics of what needed to be done and visualize the outcome. She asked smart questions and kept asking until she understood. She was well versed in the details of the contract and he soon found that she was a tough negotiator. By the time they were done a new level of respect and trust was formed between them.

"I think that covers everything," she said. "Do you?"

He nodded. "I can't think of anything that we missed. Of course, once the project begins you have to be prepared to make adjustments. There will always be something unforeseen that will spring up."

"I totally understand. As long as you keep me aware of any changes and problems."

"You have my word." He pointed at the contract. "And you have it in writing. I'll have my business partner, Max, take a look and get these back to you... tomorrow afternoon. If that works for you."

She gathered her things and stood. She looked at him for a moment. "Tomorrow is fine."

"I'll walk you out. Maybe I can introduce you to Max before you leave."

Trevor knocked but got no answer. "Hmm. Must have gone out."

"Another time. I'm sure we'll all be seeing a great deal of each other in the coming months."

He opened the front door for her and they stepped outside.

Dominique turned toward him. "Thank you for agreeing to do this. It will mean a lot to so many women."

"I'm looking forward to it."

She offered a tight smile. "Tomorrow, then." She walked off toward her car.

Trevor reigned in his urge to watch her walk away and returned back inside.

Chapter 9

Dominique parked her car in front of her office building. She was thoroughly pleased with herself. She'd eaten a little crow and it didn't taste as bad as she'd expected. Why it mattered what Trevor Jackson thought of her still eluded her. It simply did.

Spending the prior evening with him—although it ended on a sour note—and then again today only solidified her objective. She wanted him every which way but loose and she would have him. It was only a matter of time.

"How did the meeting go?" Phyllis asked the instant Dominique walked through the door.

Dominique plopped her fire-engine-red Birkin tote on the reception desk. "Perfect, of course. I made him an offer he couldn't refuse." She smiled in triumph.

Phyllis gave her a wry grin. "I'm not sure I want to know what that means."

Dominique clasped Phyllis's hands between her own. She leaned forward and whispered, "My virtue is still in tact in a manner of speaking."

Phyllis pursed her lips. "What am I going to do with you?"

"People have been asking that million-dollar question for years." She kissed Phyllis on the cheek. "I have some calls to make. How many clients today?" she asked, moving smoothly into business mode.

"Three. They will be here in an hour."

"Great. I'll do the half-hour talk with them, get a needs assessment and then you can take them through the merchandise."

"Have you thought anymore about hiring some more staff?"

Dominique frowned for a moment. Phyllis was her only full-time employee. They had two interns from the local college that came in to help out from time to time. But with the new direction that the business was taking, they were going to have to hire at least one full-time staffer along with the instructors.

"To be honest, no. I've been so focused on staffing for the classes and getting the contract taken care of…"

"That's why you have me. I've gone through the resumes and narrowed down the pool to three. They're on your desk."

"Have I told you lately that you're amazing?"

"Not since yesterday."

"Oh, then you're not due for another one until the end of the week."

"Figures."

Dominique blew a kiss, grabbed her purse and headed to the back and her office. All in all it had been a very good day.

Trevor and Matt had gone over the contract line-by-line the day before. Their attorney had given them the final okay that morning. Dominique had done her homework. She'd allowed for every contingency, the budget was solid and the time frame was reasonable. Everything that they'd discussed and agreed to verbally was included in the contract. Once they signed and got her signature, they'd get the start-up check and the work would begin.

"I still wish I had been here to see your head do a complete three-sixty," Max said before scrawling his signature next to Trevor's.

"Not funny."

"This Lawson lady must be something."

She is. "After thinking it over it was a sound business decision."

Max tossed him a skeptical glance. "Right." He pushed up from his seat, checked his watch. "I'm going to go over to the Morgan property. The plumbing is going in today."

"Cool. I have some things to take care of here." He paused. "Then I figured I'd drop off the contract, get the ball rolling."

"I can take it. It's on my way."

"Naw. I'll take care of it. Let me know what's happening on the site."

Max bit back a chuckle and slowly shook his head.

He got to the office door, stopped and turned back. "I'll show you mine if you show me yours."

"It's not what you think," he called out. "It's business."

"Of course." Max closed the door behind him.

Dominique was finishing up her session with the two new clients when Phyllis poked her head into the conference room.

"Sorry to interrupt. Mr. Jackson is here."

Dominique's fingers fluttered to her throat. A warm flush infused her. "Um, tell him I'll be right out."

Phyllis smiled. "I definitely will." She closed the door and returned up front.

"Ms. Lawson will be with you in a moment. She's finishing up a session with two of our new clients."

"Session?"

"Yes, every woman who is referred to us has a sit down with Dominique. She talks to them about their lives, their needs, their goals and how dressing for success can get them on their way. The centerpiece is self-esteem. All of the women who come here are broken in some way, have had the essence of who they are crushed. Our goal is to help them get it back."

"With clothes? I don't mean to sound skeptical but…"

"Ever hear the saying, 'the clothes make the man?'"

"Sure."

"They make the woman, too. When you look good, you feel good. Of course, it's only a small part of the healing process, but it's a start, and Dominique is masterful at what she does."

The click of heels against the hardwood floors turned them both in the direction of the sound.

It was like seeing her for the first time all over again. That same tightening in his groin as he watched her legs bring her closer. The rise of her breasts nestled in the fitted white blouse begged him to caress them. Her smile was an open invitation to heaven.

"Mr. Jackson." She extended her hand and looked up into his eyes. "This is a pleasant surprise."

He took her hand, holding it longer than necessary. "I brought over the contracts. I should have called. There was no need to interrupt your session."

Dominique's heart pounded. He was like a chameleon, shifting from raw and rugged and runway sleek apparently without any effort. Who was the real Trevor Jackson, the man in front of her or the one who sat opposite her last night? Did it matter?

"We were finishing up. Umm, would you like to come to my office?"

"I've taken up enough of your time." He handed her the manila folder with the contracts.

She took the envelope and held it against her chest. "I'll get it signed and prepare your check. I'll call you when it's ready."

He watched the pulse beat at the base of her throat. "Works for me." He took a step back.

He watched her glossed lips part, saw a hint of her pink tongue and wondered how it would taste.

Dominique's glance slid toward Phyllis who was standing to the side taking the exchange all in. "I'll call you," she finally said with an extra lift to her voice.

"I'll look to hearing from you." He turned to Phyllis. "Good seeing you again." He walked out.

It was Phyllis's loud clearing of her throat that finally broke through Dominique's trance. Her head snapped toward Phyllis. Both her brows were raised and a tsk-tsk was on her lips.

Dominique held up her hand. "Don't say it."

"I wasn't going to say a word."

Dominique planted her hands on her hips.

"Be careful, Dom. He's not like any of the men you're used to."

"All men are the same, Phyllis."

"Yes, all the men that you've dealt with. Not him." She tilted her head toward the door. "Don't make that mistake."

"Oh, Phyllis, I can handle myself. You worry too much." She spun away. "I'm going to send the ladies out."

"He's something to worry about," Phyllis murmured.

"Dom, I'm telling you getting involved with an employee is asking for trouble," Zoe was saying into the phone.

"It'll be all right. I don't have a problem with it."

"You should! Why him of all people?"

Dominique pouted. "There's something about him, Zoe. I can't explain it."

"Maybe it's the fact that he's not running after you like every other man you meet. Did it occur to you that maybe he has someone in his life already?"

Dominique tapped her foot beneath her desk. She

refused to believe that. "I saw how he looked at me. I know that look."

Zoe blew out a frustrated breath. She knew that once Dominique made up her mind about something, it would take a nuclear blast to throw her off course. "Be careful, Dom. I think you're asking for trouble."

"Come on, Zoe, you're starting to sound like Phyllis. I thought you and my sisters wanted me to find someone. Settle down." She rocked her foot a little faster.

"Of course we do, but…look, you're a grown woman. Just don't let me have to say I told you so."

"You won't."

"Take care, sweetie."

Slowly Dominique hung up the phone. Her confession—so to speak—to her sisters was that she'd "found" someone—a Trevor Jackson someone. She just happened to neglect to mention that he was her contractor.

It didn't matter. They were both firmly ensconced in Washington and wouldn't be back for months. By the time she saw them again, Trevor would be all hers and it wouldn't matter what he did for a living. She wouldn't be teased about her string of men. She wouldn't have to listen to them sigh and moan about how great love was and what she was missing.

She looked at the signed contracts on her desk and reached for the phone. By the time she saw her sisters again she wouldn't be the outsider.

Chapter 10

Trevor had been to Bottoms Up before. The food was great, the atmosphere laid back, service was polite and there was usually some solid live entertainment. It was casual chic, which was why he was taken by surprise that this was where Dominique wanted to meet for a celebratory drink to toast the signing of the contract.

He stepped into the dimly lit interior and was greeted by real laughter, music that could be heard above a whisper, the click of glasses and the scrape of forks against plates. The customers were an eclectic blend of the after-work crowd and the mid-week daters. In other words: average.

Now this was more like it.

"Good evening. Trevor, right?"

Trevor quickly took in the image in front of him. A

slow smile of recognition lifted the corner of his mouth. He pointed a finger at her. "Michelle?"

"Right." She laughed. "How are you? It's been a while since you've stopped in."

"What I am is impressed that you'd remember me. You must see hundreds of customers in a week."

She smiled. "It's my job. And some of our guests leave more of an impression than others." She paused a moment. "Can I get you a table or do you just want to hang out at the bar?"

"I'll find a spot at the bar."

"If you need anything, just ask. Enjoy your evening."

Trevor watched Michelle walk away and didn't miss the extra sway that she put in her hips. He chuckled then wound his way around bodies and tables until he reached the bar. Peering over heads and shoulders he found a seat near the end.

"What can I get ya?" the bartender asked. He wiped the spot in front of him with a white towel.

"Hennessey on the rocks."

"You got it."

Trevor reached for the bowl of nuts and scooped up a handful. He glanced around. The place was pretty packed for the middle of the week. There were a few tables that were still vacant. But from his vantage point he could tell it wouldn't last long. There was a line forming at the hostess counter.

He tossed a couple of nuts into his mouth and chewed slowly. Bottoms Up was a pretty popular lounge. The few times that he'd come it was always crowded, but that didn't diminish the service or the entertainment.

He thought he remembered something about a second location opening up somewhere, but he couldn't remember where.

This meeting with Dominique was scheduled for seven. It was coming up on six-thirty. He'd intentionally arrived early to give himself a chance to relax and unwind before sitting across the table from Dominique again.

The waiter returned with his drink.

"Thanks." He stirred it slowly with the short, red plastic straw then took a quick sip.

He'd been antsy about the meeting all day. It certainly wasn't a date, but it was a starting over of sorts. For reasons that escaped him, it mattered what Dominique thought of him. Silly, he knew that. After all, this was purely a business relationship. But he didn't want to start off on the wrong foot with a client. That made for a tension-filled working relationship. That's what he told himself. It sounded logical.

"Sure I can't get you a table?" Michelle sidled up next to him.

Trevor turned to his right. "With this crowd?" He sipped his drink, looking at her above the rim.

"Since I run the place…" She smiled.

"Oh. I had no idea."

"I took over the running of this location when Spence decided to set up the second location in D.C."

Trevor nodded. Now he remembered. "Right. He got married or something."

Her smile tightened. "Yes. To Desiree Lawson."

Inwardly, he jerked. Desiree Lawson. That had to

be Dominique's sister. He briefly remembered reading about the wedding, but until now didn't make the connection.

"Michelle…"

Michelle's eyes narrowed every so slightly. "Dominique. Good to see you…again." She started to turn her attention back to Trevor.

"Sorry if I kept you waiting, Trevor. A last-minute conference call."

Dominique was stunning as usual. Trevor felt himself stir just looking at her. The starched white blouse was opened enough to tease. Her narrow hips and shapely rear were encased in some kind of black form-fitting leggings than disappeared into a pair of forest-green suede ankle boots. The word edible came back to his mind.

Dominique turned her full-watt smile on Michelle. "Is my regular table available?"

Michelle gritted her teeth. The rivalry between her and Dominique—and by default, Desiree—Lawson went way back. The connecting link was Spence Hampton. Although it was now a non-issue, Michelle and Spence had mended the fence and she was resigned to the fact that he chose Desiree over her. But that still didn't take the bad taste out of her mouth about Dominique. The woman simply rubbed her the wrong way. And here she was again, all up in her face.

"Let me check. Good talking with you, Trevor. Come back soon." She walked away.

Dominique rolled her eyes and plopped her purse on the bar counter.

"What was that about?"

Dominique slid her glance toward Trevor. "What? That?" She pursed her lips. "Old news."

"Didn't seem like it."

"Maybe I'll tell you about it one day." She smiled up at him. "But not tonight. Tonight we celebrate the start of a productive business relationship." She reached into her purse and pulled out an envelope and handed it to Trevor. "Your signed contract and your check."

"Your table is ready, Ms. Lawson," said a young woman who was holding two menus.

"Thanks, Karen."

Karen led them to their table and Trevor took private pleasure in walking behind Dominique.

This was all a flight of fantasy, Trevor mused as he helped Dominique into her seat. There was no way he would ever get with a woman like Dominique Lawson, no matter how utterly tempting she was.

"What are you drinking?" Dominique asked.

"Hennessey."

"Hmm. I'll try one also, Karen." She focused on Trevor. "I usually go for an apple martini. But today is a day of new beginnings."

She smiled at him and he momentarily forgot his mantra that this was just business.

Karen returned with Dominique's glass of Hennessey and placed it in front of her. "Do you want to order an appetizer?"

"Please tell me that crab cakes are on the menu."

Karen grinned. "They certainly are."

She turned her brilliance on Trevor. "They are to

die for. You will be forever in my debt once you taste these."

Trevor laughed out loud. "You twisted my arm." He looked up at Karen. "I guess we'll start with the crab cakes."

Dominique raised her glass and Trevor did the same. "To new beginnings," she said.

Trevor touched his glass to hers. "New beginnings."

"And just to show you that I mean it, the tab tonight is on you." Dominique laughed and took a swallow of her drink.

This meeting was nothing like their last. Trevor felt relaxed and not out of his element and it was reflected in his repartee with Dominique. They found that they both enjoyed the Showtime series Dexter and were fans of author Harlan Coben. Dominique had traveled to places that Trevor only read about but she wasn't pompous about it, only matter-of-fact. She asked him questions about where he grew up and why he decided to do what he did for a living and he told her all about his uncle.

As he listened to her speak so passionately about her work and how she'd finally found something that she was good at, he slowly began to see her as more than a spoiled rich girl. And he knew he shouldn't because it would be too easy to get involved with Dominique.

It was nearly ten by the time they finished up dinner and started for the exit.

Trevor held the restaurant door open for her. "I'll walk you to your car."

"Oh, I didn't drive today. My car is in the shop. I'd planned to take a cab."

"No. That's crazy. I can drive you home."

Her gaze settled on him for a moment. "If you're sure. I mean, you don't have to."

"My mama brought me up better than that, I'll drive you home. My car is at the end of the block."

His black Range Rover was a big vehicle but it barely seemed to have enough room for the two of them.

Trevor swore he felt every breath she took. The scent of her clouded his thoughts. From the corner of his eye he caught glimpses of the rise and fall of her chest. He forced himself to concentrate on driving and not her soft humming to a Jill Scott tune.

Where had all of her witty chatter gone? She couldn't get a thought straight in her head. She hadn't been able to put a sentence together since she told him her address. Maybe it was the two drinks that she'd consumed. She hummed a little more to keep her mind off of his muscled thighs beneath the soft denim and the way his long fingers curled around the steering wheel.

"The next left," she was finally able to manage.

He turned into the long, winding driveway and the Lawson mansion loomed in front of him and reality set in. This was who she really was. He pulled the Range Rover to a stop at the end of the drive. There were no lights on in the house save for the motion detector lights that illuminated on their arrival.

Dominique pushed out a breath and painted on a smile. "I really appreciate the ride." She unfastened her seat belt and turned to him. Her heart leaped when her gaze clashed with his. "You want to come in for a minute? I can fix us some coffee before you get on the road."

"Oh, I don't—"

"Aw, come on. My way of saying thanks."

He hesitated. Good sense told him to turn around and get in the car. "All right. For a little while."

Chapter 11

It was big. There was no question about that. But even so, it felt like a real home. There was a sense that these rooms had been lived in. Every magazine on the glass table was out of place. There were CDs scattered across the entertainment unit. A pair of boots sat at the bottom of the staircase with what looked to be a bag of laundry.

"Come on into the kitchen. I'll turn the pot on."

He followed her through the living space that made one want to sit back, put up their feet and toss back a beer. The kitchen on the other hand rivaled his in every way. It was a chef's palace—that's all there was to it. Now he was impressed.

"Have a seat."

He pulled out a stool from beneath the island counter and sat. "Need any help?"

Dominique glanced over her shoulder. "You're kidding, right?"

"Told you I had good home training." He rested his arm on the counter and angled his body to better see her.

She spooned the coffee into the filter. "Well, please leave me to my devices. My mom was, and my sisters are, the cooks in the family." She turned the pot on then joined him. She crossed her legs.

"You're quick to talk about the talents and achievements of your siblings. What about you?"

She glanced off. Her lips tightened ever so slightly. She shrugged. "Not much to tell. My father is a powerful senator. My older sister, Lee Ann, married a senator who is being groomed for higher office. My darling twin, Desiree—" she sighed "—married my best friend. She was always 'the good twin.'" She shrugged again. "I guess there was always a part of me that wanted my own identity. Made a mess of it most of the time." She hopped up from the stool and went to the coffeepot. "Cream and sugar?"

She reached above her to take two mugs out of the cabinets and it was like watching an exotic dancer in motion. *Did she have any idea how sensual she was when she wasn't trying?*

She swung around to face him. He blinked to attention.

"Cream and sugar?" she repeated.

He cleared his throat. "A little of both."

She prepared the two mugs of coffee and brought them to the counter.

"Thanks." He raised the cup to his lips. "You seem to have found your calling," he said, picking up the thread of their conversation.

"I suppose all my years of shopping and maxing out my credit cards and threats of being disowned finally paid off." She lowered her head and laughed lightly.

Beneath the surface of her cavalier exterior, Trevor heard the threads of insecurity run through her words which were in conflict with the woman that she presented to the world. Who was the real Dominique Lawson? Was she the one who could stroll into any restaurant, business office or high-end boutique and command the attention of any and everyone and get what she wanted? Or was she the woman in front of him with slim jeans and a white shirt, swinging her foot like a ten-year-old and looking as if she didn't have a friend in the world?

"How's the coffee?"

Her questions always seemed to startle him. "Hmm, good. Thanks." He put the cup down. "I'd better be going."

Her gaze reached out to him. "You don't have to. I mean…there's no rush or anything."

His eyes moved slowly across her face, settled for a moment on the tiny pulse at the base of her throat, imagined the soft swell beneath her blouse.

And then her hand was on his, soft as butterfly wings but with the intensity of lightning bolts.

He watched her breath catch and her eyes widen for a hot second.

"Don't go," she whispered. "At least not yet. I…I

don't want to be alone tonight. I'm so sick of rattling around in this big house by myself." She forced a smile and looked into his eyes.

As much as he knew he should, how could he possibly say no to her? "For a little while."

She beamed and squeezed his hand. "Great. Let's go in the living room. I think I have that Jill Scott CD we were listening to on the drive over."

He followed her out and made himself comfortable on the couch, while Dominique scoured through the CDs. "My brother Rafe is the music buff. If he was here, he'd tell me exactly where it was," she mumbled as she continued to flip through cases.

"Where is your brother?"

She shrugged. "Knowing Rafe, he could be anywhere." She glanced over her shoulder. "If you mean is he coming home—no. He moved out months ago. The only one living in this 'humble' abode is me. Sometimes my younger brother, Justin, pops in to do his laundry. He has an apartment on campus. Dad is home a couple of months out of the year." She held the CD up in triumph then put it in the player. "My sisters are married." She shrugged again. "That leaves me." She sauntered over and joined him on the couch. She curled her legs beneath her, propped her elbow on the couch back and rested her head in her palm. "What about you? Any sisters and brothers?"

"Naw, just me."

"Didn't you get lonely?"

"No, not really. I had friends from the neighborhood and school, and me and my mother were very close."

"Were?"

"Yeah, she passed away a few years ago."

"I'm sorry." She reached out and touched his hand and that sizzle went right up his arm again.

"I know how hard that must have been. I lost my mother almost ten years ago and I still miss her." She studied his face for a moment. "That was so different from growing up here."

He chuckled lightly. "I can imagine."

Dominique shook her head. "There was always a house full of people. Kids running around, noise, fights. My father's political and business friends seemed to always be here. And in the midst of it all my mom threw the most lavish parties." She wistfully gazed off into the distance.

"Sounds like you had a good childhood."

She turned her focus on him. "I did. Maybe that's why I'm the last holdout. I want to recapture the golden days."

Trevor thought she tried to sound offhand, but the words rang with a hint of truth. "Holding on to things that have good memories can't be all bad."

She drew in a breath. "I know it's time to move on, though. Start some new memories of my own. It's crazy to ramble around in this house alone. Scary sometimes, too."

He arched a thick brow. "Scary like in haunted?" he teased.

She grinned and playfully swatted his arm. "No, silly. Not haunted. It's just that when you're alone in a place this big, you hear every sound, every creak." She gave a little shiver. "Kind of freaks me out sometimes." She pointed a warning finger at him. "And I swear if you ever tell a soul, I'll deny, deny, deny."

Trevor pressed his hand to his chest. "Your secret is safe with me."

The music changed on the player. Dominique's eyelids fluttered closed like someone overcome with ecstasy. Her body swayed gently from side to side. "I love this song."

"Chrisette Michele, right?"

"Yes! Are you a fan?"

He threw her a sidelong glance. "You're kidding, right?"

Her expression exploded in delight. She bounced on the couch. "Get out!"

He chuckled at her reaction. "I went to her concert last month."

"So did I! Oh, my goodness. How crazy is that?"

"Small world."

"I wonder what else we've done together and didn't know about it," she said, in a tone soft and sweet.

The song changed to "If I Have My Way."

Dominique got up from the couch with her hands outstretched toward Trevor. "*This* is really my song." She angled her head to the side. "Please. Dance with me. I need to see if you're as fancy with your feet as you are with your—"

His smooth embrace cut her off. Before she could gather her thoughts she was in his arms swaying to the music.

He dared not hold her too close but he couldn't help

it. She felt too good nestled against him, as if this was something they'd done forever, as if she belonged wrapped in his arms, humming softly to the music.

The heady scent of her floated around him and made him think crazy thoughts—as if *this* was right and she wanted him as badly as he wanted her. But what could be right about any of that? She represented everything that he worked to keep out of his personal life. He couldn't go down that road again. Not to mention that she was his boss. And none of it really mattered when he could feel her heart pound in her chest and beat against his, while the tips of her fingers pressed gently into his spine.

Dominique tilted her head back and her body shuddered ever so slightly when she sunk into the pool of his eyes. Her lips parted and the tiniest sigh escaped. She cupped her hand behind his head and urged him forward. She needed to experience what those lips felt like against hers. Lips that she'd fantasized about from the moment they'd met. She wanted to get closer. Needed to feel the full length of him pressed against her, wanting her as much as she wanted him.

The music faded and slowed to an end.

Dominique could hear her own pulse pounding in her ears. He hadn't moved so she pressed closer and could feel the rise of his arousal. She lifted her head, her eyes never leaving his, and touched his mouth with hers—once, twice. She glided the tip of her tongue across his bottom lip and she'd swear she felt a tremor run through him.

His arm snaked around her waist and when he spoke

his voice was a low rumble that vibrated in her center while his gaze burned across her face. "Don't do something you'll regret." And even as he said the words he couldn't be sure if he was warning her or himself.

"Life is too short for regrets." Her thumb stroked the hard line of his jaw. "Stay…"

Don't, his good sense whispered even as he lowered his head to meet her moist waiting mouth.

Tiny explosions erupted in her stomach as a flash fire soared through her veins. His lips were soft yet firm and the tenderness of his kiss made her weak. The sudden spiral of sensations gushed in a sigh that rang out like a plea.

Trevor groaned deep in his throat and the swelling need to merge her to his body blinded him to the consequences of where he knew this kiss would lead—exactly where they both wanted it to go.

Her fingers tentatively explored the hard tendons of his back, slid along the curve of his sides and stopped at his belt loop as if a warning light had gone off.

Trevor grabbed her hips and pulled her firmly against him. "This what you wanted?" he murmured against her lips.

"Yes," she gasped.

His tongue slipped into her waiting mouth and he suckled the sweetness of it.

Dominique moaned and curved her body into his. The sound stirred him even further. She slid her hand between them, cupped his bulging erection and gently stroked it.

Sighs and groans mixed to make new music that blended with Chrisette Michele's ballad "Notebook."

Trevor's strong fingers caressed the curves of her body, the tips like hot coals searing through the fabric of her clothing as his mouth continued to explore hers and the sleek lines of her neck. His thumbs traced the underside of her breasts and her breath hitched and escaped in short bursts. Suddenly she pulled away from his kiss and out of his arms.

"Not here," she whispered. Her eyes were hot with desire. She took his hand and led him upstairs.

There was still time to back out, go the other way before he crossed the threshold and she backed away from him and began to unbutton her blouse that was dazzling white in the dim light. Or before she shrugged the blouse off her arms, let it float to the floor and then unzipped her jeans.

Maybe he should leave now, before she kicked off her boots and slid out of her pants, leaving her in nothing but lacy strings that pretended to cover all the places he longed to touch.

Or maybe he should leave before he took that first step and then another until he was right up on her and could feel the warmth of her body waft up to him in waves.

But it was too late for all of that. She'd already unfastened his buckle and he'd unsnapped her bra. She'd sucked on his bottom lip while tugging down on his zipper even as his thumbs hooked around the bands of her thong and eased it over her hips.

He would have still had time to stop if he hadn't felt

the satin of her skin beneath his fingertips and if she hadn't freed him and wrapped the cotton of her hand around him, gently stroking him until his knees grew weak.

She could stop this now, knowing that she was heading down a path of no return but she couldn't when his finger separated her folds, found her wet and wanting, and slid that finger inside her, making her cry out in need.

It was simply too late. His pants were around his ankles and he'd already stepped out of them and lifted her as if she weighed no more than a child. And she couldn't stop herself now from wrapping her legs around his waist when he carried her to the bed.

What choice did she have now but to let him place his hot mouth on her nipples that had hardened, ready for plucking? None. She offered them up, the appetizer before the main course. Her breasts ached for his touch and he knew just how she liked to be caressed—firm and steady. How did he know? The question hovered in her mind for a moment then burst into a million pieces when two fingers moved inside her then out and back in again.

She gripped the soft quilt in her fists even as her hips rose and fell in concert with his steady penetration. But he wasn't only between the heat of her legs. He was everywhere on her body at once. His mouth, his hands. How could that be? But it was and he was making her crazy.

He fought for control, but the scent of her, the feel of her, the sound of her cries had him balancing on the edge. He needed to be inside her, wrapped in her, bathed by her wet walls. But not just yet. Did she taste as good as she felt?

The air jammed in her throat when she felt the heat of his tongue flick across her clit, which leaped in response. Gently he pulled the tiny bud in his mouth and her body shuddered from the bottom of her feet to the top of her head.

Trevor pushed her legs farther apart then onto his shoulders as he suckled her, laved her, relished in her cries and the undulating of her hips.

"Please…" she moaned.

"Tell me what you want…."

"You. Now."

Reluctantly he eased back and Dominique scooted up on her bed and pulled open the drawer of her nightstand. She fumbled around inside and pulled out a sealed condom.

She looked at him with a mixture of longing and uncertainty in her eyes.

Trevor took the condom from Dominique. Tore it open and rolled it on without taking his eyes off of her.

When he was done, Dominique lifted her arms to him and like a slow motion movie he lowered himself above her body before taking her legs and curving them over the bend in his arm.

He pushed his hips forward. His stiff erection teased against her wet opening. She whimpered and raised up. He pushed—just a little bit. She sucked in air, pressed her heels against his back and urged him on.

"Ahh."

"Yessss."

"So tight…my God…so tight," he moaned in her ear. His head spun. The feeling was so intense. "Hot…"

Dominique wound her hips and Trevor shuddered. He pushed, met the slightest resistance and then thrust forward all the way, as far inside as her body would allow. That instant, that moment was so powerful that neither of them dared move. To do so would change everything, make this first time no more and they wanted to remember this feeling forever.

But need, and longing, and nature took over and they had no choice but to give into the lust that had been brewing between them like a volcano ready to erupt.

Trevor scooped his hands beneath Dominique's hips and pulled her flush against him. Rising to his knees he slowly worked her up and down on his shaft.

She couldn't think, only feel the thrusts that set off electric charges that exploded in her belly and sizzled through her limbs. It was so good, so good, there were no words. All she could do was whimper and moan in delight.

Trevor tugged on his bottom lip with his teeth to keep from hollering. She was doing things with her insides—milking him—that were driving him crazy. He knew he couldn't hold out much longer, but he didn't want it to end. Ever.

He lowered her legs. She bent them at the knee. He braced his weight on his forearms and gazed down into her eyes. He knew he was lost then. There was no turning back.

Her fingers tenderly caressed his face, even while

her hips moved in slow, erotic circles. She lifted her head from the pillow, slid her hand behind his head and brought those sweet lips to hers. Her tongue darted in and out of his mouth, teased and tasted as their rhythm increased. The beat grew louder and faster.

The room grew smaller, pushing them together. The air tightened around them. The sounds of their loving rose and enveloped them.

Dominique's body jerked and stiffened. The bottom of her feet sizzled and that hot tingle raced up her legs, shook her inner thighs. A cry rose from the center of her being but hung in her throat when that first powerful spasm of release rocked her, followed by another and another. Tears sprung from her eyes. The ecstasy was surreal.

Trevor was tugged into her whirlpool. He stroked through every squeeze and release. He'd never felt this full, this hard, this crazy. He tried to pull out, to prolong the delight, but just as the tip was on the threshold of her opening, the muscles squeezed.

An animal-like cry gushed from his lungs and he plunged into her depths—once, twice and came in an explosion that rocked him to his core.

Chapter 12

Dominique listened to the water in the shower and promised that she wouldn't cry. She curled onto her side and pressed her fist to her mouth. Right now they should be cuddling and telling each other how wonderful the experience was. Her body still tingled and the pulse between her thighs beat like a drum. But she felt stupid and used instead of euphoric and treasured. There was no one to blame but herself. She'd thrown herself at him, begged him to stay, seduced him. What did she expect?

The water stopped. She sniffed hard, blinked back her tears and wiped the corners of her eyes. The door opened.

Trevor stepped out into the semi-darkened room, studied his belt buckle as he fastened it closed and looked around for the rest of his belongings. *Whatever it took not to look into her eyes.*

Dominique sat up in the bed with the quilt pulled to her chin. "Your shirt is on the floor if that's what you're looking for."

The dismissive tone of her voice grated against him.

"Yeah, thanks." He picked up his shirt and tugged it on, stepped into his shoes and checked his pockets. He dared to take a glance at her and his heart squeezed in his chest. She appeared so soft and vulnerable and there was something like need that flickered in her eyes. And then she looked away, picked up her cell phone from the nightstand and began to check for whatever. He didn't care. It was clear that she had no more need for him.

"Are you going to lock up?"

"I can set the alarm from up here," she said, still playing with her phone. "Just be sure to pull the door tight behind you."

He felt as if he'd been kicked in the gut. "No problem." He stormed out and jogged down the stairs. He couldn't get away from Dominique and that house fast enough.

The sound of the slamming door vibrated through her and pushed the tears out of her eyes. She leaped out of bed and darted to the window that looked out onto the driveway. She could see the swath of headlights, hear the engine turn over before the Range Rover was shifted into gear and pulled off.

For several moments she stood silhouetted in the window, a forlorn image that Trevor glimpsed as he drove away, an image that plagued him in his dreams for the rest of the night.

* * *

"So, how did it go last night?" Max asked, leaning against the frame of Trevor's office door with a mug of coffee in his hand.

Trevor barely looked up. "Fine."

"Yeah, I, uh, called you last night, around eleven. Guess you turned in early."

"Guess so."

Max stepped into the office and quietly shut the door behind him. As usual he was dressed for a cover shoot in a slim-fitting Italian suit of midnight-blue.

"You want to tell me what's bugging you?"

"Not really." He went to the next screen on his computer and made some adjustments to the images.

"Okay. So, when do we start the Lawson job?"

Trevor's teeth clenched. "Monday."

Max nodded, took a sip of his coffee. "Anything you need me to take care of? I have a meeting in New Orleans in a couple of hours."

"No. Got a few guys to come in to do the demo, first thing Monday morning. I'll take a look when they're done and take it from there."

"All right. Just make sure I get the list of everyone that's on the site, so I can set up the payroll."

Trevor nodded.

Max waited a few minutes, hoping that his friend would say something that had some meaning, but he walked away disappointed.

Trevor finally glanced up. He was being a jerk. Max was his best friend. They talked about everything, but

Dominique was different. It was a tender spot on his spirit that he didn't want touched.

Everything about getting involved with Dominique Lawson was wrong; wrong from the beginning. He should have paid attention to his gut and not his libido.

Sleeping with the boss! How cliché is that? Not that he could say that they actually *slept* together since he was out of there before the sheets cooled.

He blew out a frustrated breath and slowly shook his head. Stupid. How was he ever going to look her in the face after last night? It was clear from her demeanor that it was no more than a roll in the sack for her. How many other men had she spread bread crumbs for only to dismiss them with the back of her hand when she was done?

He'd believed to the pit of his soul that something beyond sex had connected them last night. He'd been with his share of women—but never like that. It was… like the first time. He shook his head.

But no matter what he thought he felt, how much she turned him on, he should have known better. He did know, but he let the smaller head make his decision. Now he was screwed, literally and figuratively. He shut his eyes for a moment and the naked image of Dominique standing framed in her window loomed behind his lids. His penis jerked to attention.

He shook his head to clear it, pushed back from his desk and stared off into the distance. She was under his skin. There was no two ways about it. He had to get her out—and fast.

* * *

Dominique walked slowly down the aisle of dresses and skirts, rearranging sizes and colors. At least that's what she thought she was doing until Phyllis's firm hand gripped hers.

"You need to stop. Right this minute."

Dominique frowned. "What are you talking about?"

"You done rearranged the sizes. You have the eights mixed in with the twelves." She pulled a suit from the rack. "This belongs on the other side." She stared at Dominique. "What is bothering you? You look like you haven't slept."

Dominique released a soft sigh. Her mouth tightened. "I didn't."

"Why, sweetie?"

Her lids fluttered like birds wings when she looked into Phyllis's warm brown eyes that reminded her of her mother's. She broke down and cried.

"Oh, my goodness…" Phyllis wrapped an arm around Dominique and ushered her to the back office. She guided her to a chair and Dominique numbly sat down.

Dominique covered her face with her hands. Her words come out muffled. "I'm sorry. I don't know what's wrong with me." She sniffed and cried some more.

Phyllis held her and let her get her tears out. Dominique tried to put on the tough exterior and cover up her insecurities and loneliness behind a high octane lifestyle and a string of men—none of whom ever got beyond first base. Which probably accounted for why they didn't last very long, Phyllis had surmised. Dominique discarded men the way most people got rid of old clothing—kindly but permanently. Even her sisters and her best friend, Zoe, didn't know the truth about Dominique. She'd entrusted Phyllis with her most precious secret and that created a special bond between them that they both treasured.

"I…I made a stupid mistake."

"What sweetheart?"

Dominique wiped her eyes and rested her head on Phyllis's shoulder. "I made love with him."

Phyllis's heart thumped. "Him?" But she knew the answer before Dominique said his name.

"Trevor." Her shoulders shook.

"It's all right," she soothed.

"It's not all right! I ruined everything. But I thought… I just thought…" Her sobs drowned out her words.

"Sssh. Hush now."

"I'm so tired of pretending, Phyllis. Tired of acting like I'm some femme fatale and worldly about life and love. I get my training from the *Housewives* reality show." She laughed sadly. "And listening to my sisters and Zoe." She lowered her head.

"Your mother and father were perfect examples of real love and how to build a lasting relationship. That's what you've always told me."

"But I'm not my mother. I never will be. I don't have what she had." She gazed off. "Sometimes I would watch my mom weave her spell around my father and he was putty in her hands. It was nothing special that she did, just the way she could say his name or look at him or touch his face."

"Sounds more like a man who loved a woman very much," Phyllis said softly.

"I suppose. I've seen Lee Ann do it with Preston and Desiree with Spence." Her shoulders slumped. "It's magic."

"It's love, Dominique."

"That's all I ever wanted, too. That magic. To have a man look at me the way my father looked at my mother. The way Preston looks at Lee Ann and Spence at Desiree and Jackson at Zoe."

"You will when the right man comes along."

"He did. And I blew it."

"First, how do you know he's the right man?"

She looked into Phyllis's eyes. "Because of the way I feel inside…long before he touched me," she said, her voice a wondrous whisper. "I've never felt that way before. And I know I saw it in his eyes. It was more than lust, like all the others…it was something else. Something more."

"If all that is true, Dominique, then why do you think you messed it up?"

The tears welled in her eyes again. "I…I was so afraid afterward…that he would know…so I acted like it was no big deal, like I didn't really care. And he left. He barely said a word."

"Oh, honey." She pulled her close.

"I don't know how to fix it."

Phyllis gently rocked her back and forth. She didn't have a solution, either.

Chapter 13

Dominique made herself put one foot in front of the other until she knew she could no longer keep up the front. Exhaustion gripped her and wouldn't let her loose. Trying to keep her game face on with less than two hours sleep had finally taken its toll.

"I think I'm going to head home, Phyllis. My eyelids feel like they weigh a ton." She stifled a yawn with the back of her head.

"No problem. The intern is coming this afternoon and I can close up."

"Thanks." She started for the door, stopped and turned back. "And thanks for this morning. I know I was a babbling brook of craziness, but I really appreciate you listening to me."

"Anytime. Now you go home and get some rest. Remember that things always look better in the morning."

Dominique gave a halfhearted smile. "See you tomorrow."

She stepped outside. The cool late-morning air did her good as she walked around back to her car then remembered that she hadn't driven. She'd decided against taking Rafe's car that he'd left in the garage and taken a car service, certain that her vehicle would be delivered today. She checked her watch. It was barely noon. She huffed in mild frustration, went back around to the front and decided to walk for a while. Maybe the walk would help to clear her head.

Dominique hooked her purse on her shoulder and strolled along Fontaine, stopping periodically to peek in the windows of her favorite shops.

Slowly the streets began to fill with early lunchgoers and Dominique knew it was time to make an exit-somewhere. She was not up for crowds today.

She turned off Fontaine and saw her aunt Jacqueline step out of the medical plaza building.

"Aunt Jacquie…"

"Oh…Dom." She faltered for a moment. Her eyes darted around then settled on her niece. She leaned over and kissed her cheek.

"I thought you'd gone back to L.A."

"I'd planned to, but something came up."

"Where are you staying?"

"At the Marriot."

"A hotel? Aunt J. You could have stayed at the house."

She shook her head. A sad smile tugged at her mouth. "You're sweet. But I'm sure your father wouldn't

An Important Message from the Publisher

Dear Reader,

Because you've chosen to read one of our fine novels, I'd like to say "thank you"! And, as a special way to say thank you, I'm offering to send you two more Kimani™ Romance novels and two surprise gifts—absolutely FREE! These books will keep it rcal with true-to-life African American characters that turn up the heat and sizzle with passion.

Please enjoy the free books and gifts with our compliments...

Glenda Howard
For Kimani Press™

W e'd like to send you two free books to introduce you to Kimani™ Romance books. These novels feature strong, sexy women, and African-American heroes that are charming, loving and true. Our authors fill each page with exceptional dialogue, exciting plot twists, and enough sizzling romance to keep you riveted until the very end!

KIMANI ROMANCE...LOVE'S ULTIMATE DESTINATION

Your two books have combined cover price of $12.50 in the U.S. $14.50 in Canada, but are yours **FREE!**

We'll even send you two wonderful surprise gifts. You can't lose!

THE EDITOR'S "THANK YOU" FREE GIFTS INCLUDE:

Two Kimani™ Romance Novels
Two exciting surprise gifts

YES! I have placed my Editor's "thank you" Free Gifts seal in the space provided at right. Please send me 2 FREE Books, and my 2 FREE Mystery Gifts. I understand that I am under no obligation to purchase anything further, as explained on the back of this card.

PLACE FREE GIFTS SEAL HERE

168/368 XDL FMQS

Please Print

FIRST NAME

LAST NAME

ADDRESS

APT.#   CITY

STATE/PROV.   ZIP/POSTAL CODE

Thank You!

The Reader Service - Here's How It Works:

BUSINESS REPLY MAIL
FIRST-CLASS MAIL   PERMIT NO. 717   BUFFALO, NY

POSTAGE WILL BE PAID BY ADDRESSEE

THE READER SERVICE
PO BOX 1867
BUFFALO NY 14240-9952

NO POSTAGE
NECESSARY
IF MAILED
IN THE
UNITED STATES

If offer card is missing write to: The Reader Service, P.O. Box 1867, Buffalo, NY 14240-1867 or visit www.ReaderService.com

appreciate me staying in his house, even for a short time."

Dominique touched her arm. "I wish things were different between you and dad."

Jacqueline pulled in a long breath. "So do I."

Dominique noticed for the first time a lack of sparkle in her aunt's eyes. She looked tired or troubled, Dom couldn't be sure. Dominique hooked her arm through her aunt's. "Well, I'm off for the rest of the day. Do you have plans?"

"Not really. I was going to grab something to eat and head back to the hotel."

Dominique grinned. "Let's do lunch. Just us girls."

Jacqueline laughed. "I'd like that."

"So would I."

"This is your town. Lead the way."

Dominique selected one of her favorite bistros and they opted to eat outside.

The waitress brought them menus. They ordered grilled salmon salads and iced teas.

"Heard from the newlyweds?" Jacqueline asked.

"Desi stopped in for a surprise visit last weekend with Lee Ann. We hung out like old times."

Jacqueline smiled. "That's good to hear. It was like that with my brothers and me. We used to call ourselves the Three Musketeers." She glanced off to the distance. "Long time ago," she said on an empty note.

Dominique reached across the table and covered her aunt's hand. "How long are you planning to stay in Baton Rouge?"

Jacqueline sighed. "Maybe another few weeks. I have…some things to take care of before heading back home."

"I'm in that big house all by myself. I'd love the company and—" she held up her hand to forestall her aunt's protest "—Daddy rarely comes home. Especially at this time of year. He stays in D.C." She leaned forward. "Please."

"Dom…I don't think—"

"I want you to. It's the family house and you're family."

The waitress returned with their food.

Dominique spread a napkin on her lap. "Aunt J, when I ran into you, you were coming out of the medical plaza building. Is everything okay?"

Jacqueline reached for her glass. She took a swallow of iced tea. "Fine."

Dominique studied her for a moment. She took a bite of her salad. "What's your next assignment?"

"There's a project in Nigeria. I'm supposed to leave next month."

"You have such an exciting life. You've photographed places all over the world. I have your latest book. The photos are incredible."

Jacqueline smiled. "Thank you. I love what I do."

"It shows." Dominique put her folk down. "Aunt J… has there ever been anyone…special in your life? Someone that could make you settle down?"

Jacqueline angled her head to the side. "What makes you ask me that?"

"I was thinking about the conversation we had at the

Desiree's wedding reception." She looked at her aunt, hoping for what, she wasn't sure. But her aunt was a woman that she admired, patterned herself after—at least she thought she had.

"Can I be honest with you?"

"Of course."

Jacqueline lowered her head just a bit then looked across at Dominique.

"I've been so busy living this life that I thought was important and amazing that the things that were really important passed me right by. They didn't wait for me to slow down." Her eyelids fluttered. "But we make choices in life." She forced a smile. "What are you trying to figure out?"

"Trying to decide what choice to make."

The corner of Jacqueline's mouth quirked upward. "Knowing you, you'll make the right choice."

"You think so?"

"I know so. And you know what else?"

"What?"

"I think I'll take you up on your offer."

"Really?" She beamed.

"Yes. Really."

"After lunch, let's head over to the hotel and get your things."

Trevor finished loading the materials onto the truck, checked with the six-man crew and they pulled off.

Demolition was scheduled to begin this morning. He'd looked forward to it and dreaded it at the same

time. Today would be the first time he'd seen Dominique since that night at her house.

More than once he'd picked up the phone to call her
but never got beyond the first three numbers. No matter
how many times he'd gone over that night in his head,
he still could not pinpoint why things went so haywire.
It didn't make sense no matter how many times he rearranged the pieces.

Then again, maybe it did. They both knew what
they were getting into was a bad idea the instant that it
started. Need overrode common sense.

Trevor pulled the company truck into the early-
morning traffic. Why, if that's all it was—a hot roll in
the sack between two consenting adults—couldn't he
stop thinking about Dominique? Why did he feel that
something more than sex had happened between them?
The question that tormented him more was: What was
she thinking and feeling? Did it mean anything at all
to her?

A car horn blasted behind him. He glanced up. He
was sitting at a green light. He put his foot on the ac-
celerator and sped across the intersection.

He understood that he still had relationship issues
because of what happened between him and Vallyn.
Maybe that was part of what went wrong the other
night. He gripped the steering wheel. But that wasn't
all of it. Afterward he could feel her withdraw. Her heat
turned cold. And his old wounds reopened. All he could
do now was stay away from Dominique Lawson and
get the job done as quickly as possible. Besides, he'd
probably never see her, anyway. She wasn't the kind of

woman that would care to be around all the dust, dirt and sweat.

The three-truck caravan pulled up in front of First Impressions. Trevor signaled for them to follow him around back where they could park.

"You guys can start unloading," he called out. He walked around to the main entrance and inside. The bells over the door jingled.

Phyllis came from behind the front counter. "Mr. Jackson. Good morning. All ready to start?"

"Yes, ma'am. They guys are out back." He glanced around as he spoke. "Can you open the door so they can start bringing the equipment upstairs?" No sign of Dominique.

"First, call me Phyllis." She reached into a drawer beneath the counter and took out a set of keys. "Ms. Lawson left these for you."

Trevor took the keys. "She's not here?"

"No. She may be in later. Did you need to speak with her? I can call her on her cell."

Why did he feel disappointed? "That's not necessary. I only needed the keys. Thanks…Phyllis."

She smiled. "If you need anything, I'll be here."

He nodded and started toward the back to open up.

"Oh, Mr. Jackson—"

He turned, a half grin on his face. "Trevor…"

"Trevor. How many men do you have with you?"

"Six."

"Fine. I'll be ordering lunch. I needed to know for how many."

"That's really not necessary."

"Dominique wanted to be sure that you all were taken care of. And when she makes up her mind, no is not an option. I'll be ordering from the deli across the street. Any preferences?"

"I'm sure whatever you decide will be fine."

"Okay, then. Shout if you need anything."

"Yes, ma'am…Phyllis."

Phyllis watched him until he turned the corner that led to the back staircase. Slowly she shook her head. She could definitely see why Dominique was so totally crazy over Trevor Jackson. That hunk was all man and a gentleman to boot.

She picked up the phone and punched in the numbers. The line rang three times before the call was answered. "He's here."

Dominique disconnected the call. Her heart was racing as if she'd been chased. She'd debated about being at the office for the past few days. Even after talking with her aunt, she hadn't dug up enough courage to face him. Not yet. Which was why she found herself parked down the street from her office instead of being in it.

She glanced down the block through her rear- and side-view mirrors. A warm heat flooded her. There he was! He looked both ways then jogged across the street. She had the ridiculous urge to duck to keep him from spotting her. He went inside the deli.

If she hurried she could get to her building and into her office without him seeing her.

She grabbed her keys and her purse, set the alarm

and started down the street. She felt like running but opted for a brisk pace instead. Her pulse was beating so fast she felt lightheaded. This was crazy!

The front door was in sight. She was less than ten feet away when she spotted Trevor coming out of the deli balancing a tray of coffee.

Maybe she could pretend that she didn't see him and simply dart inside. But as her luck would have it, they reached the entrance within steps of each other.

They tried to look everywhere but at each other and failed miserably.

"Hello," he said.

"Hi," she managed.

"We're starting the demo today."

"Right." She laughed nervously. "I almost forgot."

His eyes tightened. "Really? Phyllis mentioned that you wanted her to order lunch for the crew."

She swallowed, shifted her weight to her left. "I mean I almost forgot…how early you were going to be here." Did she just say that? His lips were moving but she wasn't paying attention. All she could think about was how they felt on her—

"Umm, can you get the door, please?" He indicated the tray of hot coffee.

She blinked. "Sure. Sorry." She pulled the door open and stepped aside. The scent of him wrapped around her and her tummy did a flip. Dominique drew in a deep breath of him and followed him inside.

Phyllis's eyes widened when she saw the two of them walk in together.

"I could have ordered that for you," Phyllis said.

"No worries." He continued to the back and upstairs.

"Well," Phyllis said in a pseudowhisper, "did you say anything?"

"I…I don't know what I said." She put her purse on the counter. "I said something…I guess."

Phyllis shook her head. "What happened to the Dominique Lawson that I've always known? When have you ever not been able to talk to a man and say what was on your mind?"

"This is different."

"Why, because you finally have feelings for someone?"

Dominique's eyes met Phyllis's probing ones. "Yes," she murmured.

"Well, if you don't want to make it more of a mess than it already is, you'd better find the old Dominique."

Chapter 14

Dominique went to her office and shut the door. The sound of heavy boots and banging vibrated over her head. She visualized Trevor pulling out walls, his muscles flexing and sweat dampening his body. Her lids fluttered closed. The image of his naked body over hers exploded behind her closed lids—the feel of him moving slowly and deeply inside of her caused an involuntary moan to spill from her lips. Her eyes flew open. She looked around as if expecting to find someone watching her secret moment.

She sighed heavily. Her aunt Jacquie told her not to let ego stand in the way of her heart nor the illusion of never needing anyone. It was the mistake she'd made in pursuit of her career and her "free-style" life. Phyllis had pretty much counseled her the same way, going as far as to say she'd let go of the very qualities that made her the unique person that she was—strong, determined and direct.

Dominique had begun to admit that they were right. She wished she could explain why she became two left feet and all thumbs when it came to Trevor. She hadn't been right from the instant he'd stepped through her office door. It was as if all her life she'd been waiting for him and then there he was and the reality was more than she could handle.

At some point she would have to make a decision to either speak up or give up. For the life of her she couldn't pinpoint what the attraction was. Of course, he was a gorgeous specimen of a man. He had a type of natural charisma that was hard to resist. Sensuality flowed through him like a rolling spring. But she'd met countless men like him before. Yet she'd never felt that "something" so deep in her soul that it stole her breath, short-circuited her thoughts and moved her to share her body.

She slapped her palms on her desk. He was a laborer for heaven sakes. He didn't travel in her circles. His livelihood depended on the next job. He wasn't on a first-name basis with entertainers, politicians and corporate executives. His name wouldn't open locked doors. That was all her world and she could never see Trevor fitting into it.

And it didn't matter. None of it did. Crazy, but it didn't matter! The flash of realization stirred inside, formed and become something she could hold on to. The weight of indecision began to lift. A slow, tentative smile pulled at the corners of her mouth. *It didn't matter.*

* * *

Trevor worked like a man possessed. He tore into walls with the fury of the gods. He barely stopped to take a breath between swings of the sledgehammer, and lifted armloads of wood alone.

He had a single purpose: work so that he couldn't think. He wanted his muscles to ache and have his body too tired to want to do anything more than go home alone to a hot bath and bed. Too tired to think about Dominique.

The noise diminished by degrees, one hammer, one voice at a time. The silence caught Trevor in mid-swing. He turned toward the direction of the silence. His insides shifted.

Dominique stood in the midst of the debris like a mirage in the Mohave. She smiled and nodded to the men as she gingerly stepped over planks of wood and buckets of plaster, racking up appreciative looks along her way to Trevor.

Even in the middle of what looked like the aftermath of a minefield detonation she'd spotted him. He pulled his work goggles off his eyes and up onto his head. The sweet chocolate of his face was coated in a light white powder—like sugar on a donut. His army-green shirt was molded to his body, outlining the bulging, defined muscles. Sweat glistened on his biceps. She had never seen anything more beautiful or magnificent.

She wasn't sure how long she'd stood there, staring, but then he was standing right in front of her, telling her it was dangerous for her to be there without a hard hat.

That wasn't the reason it was dangerous, the working half of her brain warned.

Trevor took a rag from his back pocket and wiped his face.

She took a step back and her shoe caught on a loose floorboard. She stumbled backward and the room, filled with hard-bodied men, reacted as if a starter pistol had been shot. They leaped from their places around the room but not before Trevor grabbed her arm to keep her from falling.

"Careful. Not a good place for you to be right now, Ms. Lawson."

The pressure of his fingers felt like steel bands around her arm.

Dominique looked into his eyes hoping to see the answer that she needed. But before she could probe too deeply he'd let her go and repositioned his goggles over his eyes.

"Something that you needed?" He still held the sledgehammer and was lightly swinging it by his side.

Dominique was mesmerized by the way the muscle in his arm rose and fell in rhythm to his movements. She swallowed. "Um, you said I needed a hard hat?"

His brow arched with skepticism. "You came about a hard hat?"

"You said I needed one. I wanted to take a look around at the work." She lifted her chin a notch.

"Want to make sure your money is being well spent," he said only loud enough for her to hear.

Inwardly she flinched.

"Do I *need* to check on how my money is being spent?" she snapped back.

He studied her for a moment. "Carl!" he called out over the renewed din.

"Yeah, boss."

"Get me a hard hat for the lady."

He turned to Dominique. "Until he gets back, you need to get out of the way before you get hurt."

"What do you care?"

"I don't. But you still need to get out of the way."

She felt the burn in her eyes and the constriction in the back of her throat. He would not make her cry. She wouldn't give him the satisfaction. She was the boss, damn it! He worked for *her.*

She folded her arms. "How long is the demolition going to take?"

"We should be finished this floor by the end of the day."

"Then what?"

"Clean up and start reframing the rooms according to the specs that we discussed."

She nodded and looked around.

"The electricians and plumbers will come in later in the week."

Carl returned with the hard hat. "Here ya go, boss."

"Thanks." He took the hat and handed it to Dominique.

She took it and sat it on her head.

Trevor bit back a smile. It all but swallowed her exquisite face, a face that continued to haunt him day and night. He wouldn't be able to work with her around.

That was for sure. So, the sooner he gave her the fifty-cent tour the better.

"I'll show you what we've done so far." Against his better judgment he touched her again, taking her arm to guide her around the debris. He led her to the back and somehow her hand slipped into his as they stepped over piles and the sensation shot up his arm. His jaw clenched. He cleared his throat. "We've, uh, taken down the wall that was here to open the space from front to back. This is where you wanted the computer center."

The heat from his hand rushed through her body. Her face flushed and whatever she might have said in response evaporated like morning mist. She knew he was talking, explaining, but she couldn't concentrate or make sense of it all.

Pipes and exposed brick were everywhere. Dust swirled around them.

"That's it so far."

They'd stopped walking.

"Any questions?"

She shook her head no. "I should get out of your way."

"Stop by anytime." He released her hand and the world grew cold.

She stole a glance at him. For an instant she saw in his face what she'd seen the night at her house—*desire*. Or perhaps it was her desire being reflected back at her.

"Send someone down when your crew is ready for lunch. We'll order it for you."

"It's really not necessary."

"I know. It's something I want to do. Can I, without it becoming an argument?"

He exhaled deeply. "Fine. Whatever makes the customer happy."

She turned and wound her way out.

Trevor watched her leave. He couldn't figure her out. One minute she was miss high and mighty, throwing her name and money around. The next minute she was simply a caring woman. All wrapped up in an unbelievably sexy package.

Dominique took her time going down the stairs. How was she ever going to get through the next few weeks, months, with Trevor being so close—and so cold to her? Well, if he didn't care then she wouldn't, either. She had a business to run.

Chapter 15

"So, I take it things haven't gone very well with you and Mr. Contractor." Jacqueline sat. She took a sip of wine and curled her legs beneath her on the couch.

Dominique sighed. "No, not exactly." She shook her head. "I can't seem to get myself together when I'm around him. Either I want to bite his head off or…"

Jacqueline laughed. "Sounds like you got it bad, girl."

She peeked at her aunt over the rim of her wineglass. "That ever happen to you?"

Jacqueline set her glass down on the side table. She ran her fingers through her short spirals. "Yes," she finally admitted.

"And what did you do?"

"I made the same mistakes you're making and…I lost him to someone else who was willing to be real with him." She reached for her glass to hide the hurt in her eyes.

"I'm sorry," she whispered.

"Don't be. I'm a big girl. But you have the opportunity to write a different end to the story, but only if you really want to." She adjusted herself in the seat. "Dom, you have been so accustomed to men falling over themselves to be with you that you have no idea what it's like to have to work for a relationship. It's pretty clear from what you've told me that this Trevor isn't your average guy." She paused. "But I need to ask you this."

"Okay."

"Do you want him because you really have feelings for him or because he seems unattainable?"

She sat up in her seat. "Do you think I would go to bed with a man that I didn't have feelings for?"

Jacqueline angled her head to the side. "Dom, women do it all the time. You wouldn't be the first or the last."

"But as much as people think otherwise, I'm not like that, Aunt J. I mean I act like it—all worldly and sophisticated—but I wanted to be with the right man. You know what I mean?"

Jacqueline nodded. "Of course I do."

"When I met Trevor…I'd never felt like that before. And I know I didn't give myself a chance to really know him before…but…I felt like I did. You know? There was just something…I can't explain it. I don't understand it. And seeing him every day, knowing that he's only a few feet away, it's making me crazy!" She pounded her fist into the couch. Then smiled shyly.

"Happens to the best of us, sweetheart. There's always that one—" her aunt held up a finger "—that has that sumthin' sumthin' you can't explain." She shook her head in appreciation. "Humph."

Dominique giggled. "He definitely has that."

Jacqueline finished her glass of wine. "I'm going to turn in. I have some running around to do tomorrow. Think about what I said."

"I will."

Jacqueline got up and stretched. "See you in the morning."

"Night." Dominique leaned back against the soft cushions of the couch. It had been three weeks since the renovations began. The crew was making incredible progress. The first floor was taking shape and next week they planned on doing the demo on the floor above. If she kept sitting around twiddling her thumbs, the job would be finished and Trevor would be gone. What she needed was a plan.

Trevor was carrying in a six-foot box of floor tiles on his shoulder. The plan today was to lay the new floor in the back room. Although he could use the help, he chose to do it alone and sent the rest of the crew to the second floor to finish with the demo. When he heard footsteps he started to bark out that he was fine until he saw Dominique with her hard hat, jeans, work boots and a flannel shirt.

He lightly shook his head to clear it. He couldn't be seeing correctly. Slowly he stood up.

"I came to help."

"Help?"

"Yes. I figured that this was my place and I want to participate in getting it together." She looked around. "You're working alone. I thought you could use some help and I could learn in the process."

He stared at her for an incredulous moment. "Okay, I give up. Where are the cameras? I'm being punked. Right?"

She had to laugh. "No! I'm serious. I watch HGTV and DIY all the time."

That sent Trevor into a fit of much-needed laughter.

"Are you making fun of me?" She planted her hands on her hips.

"Naw. I would never do that," he said over the fading strains of his laughter.

Dominique made a face. "So, can I help or not?"

"You sure about this?"

"Positive."

"Hmm. All right. Let's get started, then. You're gonna need some gloves." He pulled out a pair from his tool belt and handed them to her. "They may be kind of big but I don't want you to hurt your hands."

She took the gloves and slid her hand into one of them. Her fingers swam around inside. But she got a tingle all over knowing that Trevor's hands had been in them.

"That's the second time you were concerned about my well-being," she said, putting on the second glove.

"I'm concerned about everyone's safety that's on my work site. Come on, I'll show you a few things," he said before she could come back with a retort.

They started by unloading the boxes. The wood panels for the floor were a lot lighter in weight than she'd thought.

"The subfloor has already been laid to make sure that it's totally level."

"I know all about subfloors," she said with a grin.

"Hmm, from HGTV."

"Yep."

He chuckled. "You can start handing me the panels."

They worked in sync for nearly two hours, and Trevor even let Dominique lay several panels herself. He had to admit that she was a quick study and he grudgingly admired her stamina. Being on your hands and knees for hours wasn't easy on anyone. But she never complained.

"Ready to take a break?"

"I could use some water." She wiped her forehead with the back of her hand and left a smudge.

He reached out to wipe it away.

She sat motionless and then took his hand and brought it to her lips. Softly she kissed his palm. "I'm sorry," she said.

A knot tightened in his gut. "About what?"

"About that night."

"Oh. Yeah." He stood. "Forget it. I did." He started to move away.

She jumped up and clasped his arm. "I don't believe you. I didn't. And…I don't want to." Her eyes moved slowly over his face. "I can't."

His gaze narrowed. He turned to face her fully. "So, what are you saying? Exactly."

She glanced down at the floor then looked him in the eye. "I'm saying…that I want to try and see where things could go between us."

"Really. And why is that? Slumming?"

She stiffened. "Is that what you think of yourself?" she threw back.

"Maybe you should go back to your clothes and accessories before this gets out of hand."

Air caught in her chest. She glared at him, spun around and practically ran out.

Trevor stood in the middle of the half-finished floor, leaned his head back toward the ceiling and closed his eyes. *Idiot!*

Dominique shut the door to her office and fell into her club chair. She pressed her fist to her mouth as tears slid over her cheeks. So much for being honest. She sniffed and swiped at her eyes. *He's such a…* She couldn't find the word to describe him. What made her think in a million years that he was any different from any other man? It was all in her head. He didn't give a damn. She was probably just another notch in his belt of conquests. She wondered if she would now become a sordid topic of conversation over a few beers. Just the thought renewed her tears.

Now that she'd really made a complete fool of herself, she knew she could not face him again. He was probably up there laughing his behind off at her expense.

Phyllis could run the business without her for a few weeks. They had interns and she'd hired another part-timer. Until the renovations were finished and the equipment installed, it would be general business as usual.

Maybe she'd go to Atlanta and stay with Cynthia for a while. Zoe had her hands full with the kids and her husband and both her sisters were busy. She sniffed. All she knew was that she had to get away.

Her cell phone rang. She dug it out of her jeans' pocket. Her brother Rafe's name appeared. She wiped her eyes and pressed Talk.

"Hey, big brother."

"Had you on my mind. How are things going with the reno?"

Her throat constricted and before she knew what was happening she'd blurted out almost everything.

Rafe was silent for a while. "Well, sounds like you have yourself in a bit of fix, little sister."

"Something like that," she mumbled.

"Want my advice?"

"I guess."

"Give him some space. Sounds like he's walking that thin line."

"What thin line?"

"Employer and employee. A tough combination. Especially when the boss is a woman."

"You really think so?"

"Yeah. He's probably going through all kinds of hoops in his head. I know I would."

"But I told him I wanted to try to see how things go," she said in a plaintive tone."

"I know, sugah, and being a man, it probably threw

him for a loop. Although we love to have women come on to us, we still like to feel that we've in the driver's seat."

"Why do men have to be so…dumb?"

"I'm wounded."

She grinned. "No you're not."

"Give it time. The next move is up to him. If hc doesn't make it, then you will have to chalk this one up."

She sighed. "I guess. Where are you, anyway?"

"Cancun."

"Alone?"

"Of course not."

"Why did I ask? When are you coming back?"

"Couple of weeks. But if you need me, I'm only a phone call away. I can always cut my trip short and have a man-to-man talk with the brother."

"No, thank you! I can take care of myself."

"That's more like it. Well, gotta run. Duty calls." He chuckled. "Call if you need me…even if you only want to talk."

"I will. Love you."

"Love you, too."

She disconnected the call and settled back into the comfort of the chair. If anyone knew about the complexities of men, it was her brother. Hopefully he was right.

A light knock on her door stirred her. "Yes," she called out.

The door slowly opened.

She craned her neck to see who it was. "Hey, Phyllis."

"Someone here to see you." She stepped out of the frame of the door and was replaced with Trevor.

Dominique's defenses mounted along with the pounding of her heart.

Since she didn't throw anything at him or tell him to go to hell, he stepped inside and shut the door behind him.

Dominique twisted around in her seat. She gripped the sides of the chair.

Trevor crossed the room and came to stand in front of her.

She stared up at him not knowing what to expect and then he took her hands and pulled her to her feet and into his arms.

Before she could breathe his mouth covered hers. His tongue pushed inside her mouth and danced. He pulled her flush against him and she felt as if she was melting into his body.

Strong fingers rode up and down her spine, cupped her derriere and gently squeezed.

Dominique moaned into his mouth as her hands splayed across his chest. Her head spun with delight and confusion.

Trevor turned lowered himself into the chair and pulled her onto his lap. Her legs draped across the arm as she nestled against him, savoring the sweetness of his kisses.

His mouth dragged away from her and trailed down to her neck, tenderly suckling the soft skin.

Dominique whimpered when a tremor scurried down her center. Waves of sensation rolled through her and she didn't realize that he'd unbuttoned her shirt until she felt the heat of his mouth on the crest of her breasts.

"Oooh," she moaned.

"I'm sorry," he said, from deep in his throat. He pushed the cup of her bra down and sucked the right nipple into his mouth.

Dominique trembled. He tightened his hold on her. She felt the hard knot of his erection press against her. Oh, lawd, she wanted him.

And then as quickly as it began he stopped. He was breathing hard. And the almost dangerous look in his eyes was frightening.

"I only wanted to apologize." He half smiled at her stunned expression. "But if this is what you really want, we do it my way."

She sat up a bit, pulled her shirt closed in her fist. "Your way? And what way is that?"

He stood with her in his arms and then set her on her feet.

"I don't fraternize on the job for one thing."

"What do you call this?"

"A lapse of judgment."

"I see. Go on."

"We take this thing slow."

She nodded. "And?"

"If we do the fancy thing again, it will be on my dime."

She shrugged. "Fine. Anything else?"

"Be ready at eight. I'll pick you up at your place."

"What if I have plans?"

"Do you?"

"Maybe," she taunted.

He leaned down and took a last kiss that left her weak in the knees.

"See you at eight." He turned and walked out.

Her brother's words came back to tease her; *a man likes to feel that he's in the driver's seat.*

A slow smile moved across her mouth. She was more than ready for the ride.

Chapter 16

"This isn't the first time you've been on a date," Jacquie was saying as she sat on the edge of Dominique's bed while Dominique darted around her room.

"I know. It just feels like it."

"Where is he taking you?"

"I don't have a clue. He said be ready at eight."

"That's still three hours from now. You have time."

"I have no idea what to wear."

Jacquie laughed. "A woman's greatest plight. I'm sure whatever you decide will be fine." She pushed up from the bed. "Just make sure I get a peek at him before you leave."

"To give your seal of approval?" She held up a black Donna Karan dress, shook her head and put it back in the closet.

"You're damned right. I want to check out the man

who finally got my niece to pay attention." She walked toward the door. "Something simple," she suggested. "Works for any occasion." Jacqueline closed the door behind her.

Dominique stood inside her closet. Too many choices, she conceded. Maybe a nice hot bath would unwind her and clear her head.

Trevor stopped by the office before heading home and was stunned to find Vallyn waiting for him.

Her gaze zeroed in on Max who was sitting on the edge a table. Max shrugged.

"What are you doing here, Vallyn?"

Her head turned toward Max, who ignored her silent request for privacy. She faced Trevor. "I wanted to talk to you."

"I'm pretty sure we said it all a long time ago." He started to go past her.

"No. We haven't." She stood a bit straighter. "I wouldn't be here if it wasn't important."

"Whatever it is, say it and leave."

"Can I please talk to you in private?"

He tried hard to remember why he thought he was in love with her once. Nothing came to mind. "You have five minutes." He strode past her toward his office.

Vallyn walked in behind him and shut the door.

"Now, what is it?" He stood glowering at her, all the all hurts, the humiliation and betrayal roared to the surface, pounding in his ears like the surf crashing against the shore.

"May I sit?"

"Your visit isn't going to last that long."

"Then maybe you should sit."

His voice rose. "What do you want, Vallyn?"

"When I left…" she began and saw his expression tighten, "it was for a reason."

"Yeah, I know all about *him*."

"I deserve that. But that wasn't the entire reason."

"Get to the point." He walked to his drafting table and began rolling up some drawings.

"Our daughter."

He stopped cold. "What?"

"Her name is Traci. She's five. She's beautiful and smart…."

He shook his head to clear it. "What the hell are you talking about?"

"We have a daughter, Trevor. Me and you. That's why I left. My parents would have never stood by and let me have a relationship with you. You know that. When I found out I was pregnant, I knew I couldn't tell you."

He gripped the edge of the desk. "You're not making sense," he managed as he struggled to put together what she was saying. His breath came in short deep bursts. "Why are you telling me now?"

She lowered herself into a chair. "I want you to take care of her."

Dominique finally settled on a simple black skirt that showed just the right amount of knee with a silk, sleeveless top in a cool coral. She unwrapped her hair from her headscarf and styled it with her fingers.

If she knew where they were going at least she would know how to plan, she thought while she put on a light coat of lipstick. She pressed her lips together. But that was the whole point. *He* wanted to do the planning.

Not being in control was not a feeling that she was used to. Lack of control had been the case since they'd met. She hadn't been in control of her feelings, her body and now she didn't even have a say so in where they went for the night.

She stood in front of the mirror. Whether, Mr. Jackson knew it or not, the ball was back in her court. Let the games begin.

"What? You got to be kidding me." Max stared at his friend in total disbelief. He twisted his knotted tie until it hung loose around his neck.

"That's what she told me." Trevor paced the expanse of his office like a man possessed. He sat down and sprung right back up again.

"Do you believe her?"

"Man, I don't know what to believe," he said, his eyes wide. "Dammit." He slammed his fist against one of the wood pillars.

"So, what are you going to do?"

Trevor shook his head back and forth. "I...don't know. What *can* I do?"

"What can you do! Maaaan, you need to make sure the child is yours, for starters," he said, pointing his finger at Trevor. "Don't you think it's real convenient that Vallyn is back in town and drops this on you? What took her so long? She's been back for almost a month so she said. Why weren't you the first stop if this 'news' was her real agenda? Why tell you now?"

Trevor ran his hand across his head. Max's barrage of questions along with his own bounced like beach balls in his head.

"Is it possible that the child is yours, Trev?"

Trevor looked at his longtime friend. "Yeah. Real possible."

To say he was rattled by the time he pulled up in front of Dominique's house was an understatement. He'd spent more than an hour talking with Max who had taken the entire thing very personally. He'd never forgiven Vallyn for what she'd done and this only added to his blatant distaste.

He'd gone home and stood under the pounding shower until the water grew cold; he'd stepped out and his new reality slapped him in the face. He'd picked up the phone to call Dominique and cancel, but he wanted to see her, even in the middle of this colossal mess. Thinking about her soothed the rage in his soul. A few hours with Dominique would give his mind a needed reprieve.

He cut the engine, stared up at the light in the upper window and wondered what Dominique was doing right at that moment. He saw someone move past one of the windows. In a matter of hours his entire life had done a one-eighty and back again. First, the whole thing with Dominique that went from cold to hot, to cold to hotter. And then here comes Vallyn. He blew out a breath of pure exasperation and got out of the car.

His foot was on the last step of the entry landing when the front door swung open. It took him a moment to realize that it wasn't Dominique but definitely a relative. She'd said her sisters were away.

"Hello."

Her voice was like molasses—slow and sweet. "Evening. I'm—"

Deep dimples flashed when she smiled. "Trevor Jackson. Please come in. I'm Dominique's aunt Jacqueline."

She reminded him of a young Lena Horne. Trevor tipped his head. "Pleasure." He stepped inside.

"Dom will be down in a minute. Have a seat. Can I get you something to drink?"

"No, thanks." He sat down on the couch.

"Dominique tells me that you're in charge of the renovations."

He crossed his ankle on his knee. "Yes, I am."

"I won't beat around the bush because we don't have much time."

Trevor frowned. "Excuse me?"

"If you care about my niece, don't do anything to hurt her. She plays tough but she doesn't come close. And if you ever mention that I said anything to you I'll deny it and then you will regret it." She smiled sweetly. "Sure I can't get you anything?"

Okay, his life had now entered reality television territory. Thankfully, Dominique came downstairs. He stood and when he took her all in, all the nonsense and craziness of the day vanished. All that was left was a need to hold her and make sure that at least she was real and wouldn't shape-shift into someone that he didn't recognize.

The closer she drew with that gorgeous smile on her face, the warmer and more settled he felt. The tension eased from his shoulders and the knot loosened in his stomach. He'd made the right decision not to cancel.

"Hey," he said.

"Hey, yourself." She walked right up to him, paused for a moment then tipped up and kissed his cheek. "Sorry to keep you waiting," she said in his ear. "My aunt didn't grill you, did she?" She stepped back.

He took a quick glance over his shoulder. Jacqueline was sitting on the side chair, the picture of innocence.

"Nope."

"Good." She slipped her hand in his.

"Ready?"

She nodded. "See ya, Aunt Jacquie."

"Good night. Enjoy yourself. Nice to meet you, Trevor."

"You, too."

They stepped outside and Trevor opened the door to the Range Rover. He'd thought about taking the Porshe or the BMW convertible but decided to hold those cards until later.

"Are you going to tell me where we're going?" She fastened her seat belt.

"Hmm, nope." He turned to her and winked.

"Fine. I'm game if you are."

"And what does that mean?" He turned the key in the ignition.

"A girl has to have her secrets, too." She winked back.

He leaned over and kissed her lightly on the lips. "And I will have to see how I can make you give up the secrets."

"I'm game if you are," she said over the flutter in her stomach.

He put the car in Drive and pulled off.

Chapter 17

They drove into town and down narrow back streets that opened onto a stretch of restaurants and bars. Trevor cruised until he found a parking space.

Dominique loved this part of town. She, Zoe and her sisters spent many a night closing down some of the lounges. Before everyone got up and married, that is.

"How do you like eating crawfish with your fingers and a plastic bib?" he asked, helping her out of the truck.

"Mister, I can crawfish you under the table. Lead the way."

"Ohh, you're on, lady." He took her hand and led her down the strip to his favorite spot, Charlie's. He pulled open the heavy wood door and they were greeted with a blast of laughter, loud voices, aromatic spices and music.

"I love this place," she shouted over the din.

"As long as the waiter doesn't come over and kiss your ring we're good," he shouted back.

They were shown to a table that wobbled, but the music was great, the atmosphere was pumping and when the food came they were in heaven.

They laughed and shouted over the noise and finished off three bowls of crawfish and corn.

"I had no idea you came here," Trevor said.

"I used to come here a lot."

"You never cease to amaze me."

"Really?" She grinned. "I hope it's a good kind of amaze."

"Yeah…it is."

The music shifted from foot stomping to a slow ballad.

Trevor dipped his hand toward her. "May I have this dance, Ms. Lawson?"

"Yes, you may, Mr. Jackson."

He helped her out of her seat and led her onto the small dance floor. They swayed to the sounds of Kem's "I Can't Stop Loving You."

Dominique rested her head on Trevor's chest. The steady rhythm of his heart beat in time with hers and it was so very soothing. She closed her eyes and felt her body melt into his. This felt right. The way it should be.

Holding her like this momentarily made all of the craziness of the day fade into the background. The fit was perfect. And the more time he spent with Dominique, the more he wanted to be with her. As much as they were different, they were discovering that they had so many things in common. And once you stripped away all the airs and flamboyance, Dominique was an ordinary woman. No, ordinary was the wrong word. More like extraordinary.

The music sailed to an end.

Dominique looked up at him and smiled. "Not bad on the dance floor."

"You're not so bad yourself." He held her a little tighter. "Ready to go?"

The three words dipped down to her center and stirred. She was ready to go wherever he wanted to take her.

Trevor took care of the bill and with his arm securely around her waist they strolled back to the car.

"I had a great time. Good choice."

"Glad to hear it. It's been a while since I've been to Charlie's, as well."

"I'm surprised I never ran into you before," she said, a bit of wonder in her voice.

"What's that saying…like two ships passing in the night."

She laughed. "Yeah, something like that."

They reached the truck.

"Where to now?"

"Tired?"

"No."

He started up the engine. "Good."

Dominique sat back, ready for whatever came her way.

They drove for about twenty minutes outside of downtown when the shops and businesses became fewer and the lush neighborhoods with the towering trees and wraparound porches became more prominent.

Trevor turned the truck onto a cul de sac. There was one house at the end of the road that was bordered by a small stream.

Dominique squinted through the lamp-lit night. The area looked familiar. Not so much that she'd been here before, but maybe she'd seen this area in a photograph or on television. The house definitely rang a bell.

Trevor pulled into the drive, hopped out, came around and helped Dominique to her feet. "Here we are."

"Ooookay. And where is here?"

He grinned. "Come on inside. I'll fix you a drink and tell you all about it."

Dominique followed Trevor inside and was instantly awestruck when she stepped in. It was fabulous and manly and sexy and cozy cool all at the same time.

"Welcome to my humble abode. Make yourself comfortable."

She turned in a slow circle, taking in every inch of the tastefully stylish decor. The wide-open floor plan gave the large space a feeling of going on forever. Where her family home was pretty much contemporary, Trevor's home kicked it up a notch with a twist. It would be so easy to be comfortable here.

"Can I fix you a drink?" Trevor asked, tapping into her observations.

"Oh, yes…sure. What do you have?"

"Beer, wine, something harder…"

The *something harder* made her temperature rise. "Beer."

"Rolling Rock, cool?"

"You are kidding me! That's my favorite."

He chuckled. "Come on in the kitchen."

He went to the double-door stainless-steel refrigerator. The bottom row actually had a rack for beer. He took out two, opened them both and handed her one. "Glass or bottle?"

"Always better in a bottle."

"Now you're talking." He clicked the neck of his bottle against hers. "To surprises…"

"Surprises."

They took long cool swallows and hummed in pleasure.

"Come on, let's relax inside."

They walked back out into the living area. Trevor went to the entertainment center and shuffled through some CDs, put them on and joined her on the sofa.

The sofa had to be custom built. The back end of it actually wrapped around and hugged the curve in the wall, giving the illusion of joining the dining area with the living space. She was impressed.

"How long have you lived here?"

"Hmm, going on five years. Found it quite by accident." He took a swallow of his beer and told her the history of the house.

"Now I know why this place looked familiar. I'd seen pictures of it back in its heyday with Madame Charise. Lucky accident."

"How 'bout that. But you know when you feel something is right you have to go with your gut."

"Yeah," she said on a breath.

"So, what was it like growing up a Lawson?"

She lowered her head for a moment and laughed. "Sounds like a reality television show."

"It kinda does."

"You can read all about the antics of the Lawson family. I want to know more about you." She studied his face. "Everything." She was still having a hard time processing the blue collar Trevor Jackson that she had in her head and the persona he presented, with *this* Trevor Jackson *and* the T.J. that showed up at the Chateau looking like he was ready for a cover shoot *or* the man she'd slept with who was sexy and tender and rough and made her lose more than her mind. He was a chameleon, seemingly able to switch up at will. But who was the real Trevor?

He draped his arm casually across the back of the couch and turned halfway toward her. "Some of it you know. I grew up as an only child, raised by a single mother who worked two jobs to make sure that I never did without. My uncle was like the father I never knew. He was my inspiration for going into contracting and for going to college for my degrees."

"Degrees, as in plural?"

"Yeah." The corner of his mouth quirked. "Met Max in college. We've been friends for years. He came on board as my business partner once I got set up." He reached for his beer bottle. "That's about it." He looked at her through half-mast lids.

"No...significant others, engagements, marriages along the way?" she gingerly probed.

He drew in a breath. "Yes to the significant other and an almost engagement. Marriage zip. One out of three." He brought the bottle to his lips and finished off the beer.

"Oh. Sorry. I mean...about the engagement that didn't work out."

"No need." He put the bottle down on the table, lifted his hand from the back of the couch and played with a wisp of her hair. "If I was still engaged or married... we wouldn't be sitting here. I wouldn't be hungry to see you the way I saw you that night."

Her breath caught for a moment.

"I would be somewhere else, with someone else, doing this...." He slowly lowered his head until his mouth hovered over hers—waited. His tongue brushed across her bottom lip and he groaned when he felt her tremble. He drew her closer.

Dominique's fingers played with his chest, traveled down his hard abdomen then unfastened and unzipped his pants with an ease that surprised her.

Trevor sucked in air through his teeth when her soft fingers wrapped around him and began a steady stroking. He hadn't thought of anything else for weeks since that night at her house. Now to have her back, he was going to make sure it was a night neither of them would forget.

He gripped the fabric of the couch. "You have a change of clothes in that big bag of yours?" he managed to say.

"Why?" she breathed and flicked the pad of her thumb slowly back and forth over the swelling head.

Trevor clenched his teeth. "I intend to keep you in my bed until well after daybreak."

"Clothing has never been an issue for me." She tugged her top out of her skirt and pulled it over her head. She tossed it on the floor. She reached in front and unsnapped her bra. It followed her top.

Trevor's eyes feasted on the perfect globes that over-flowed just a bit in the palms of his hands. His finger-tips grazed the hardened buds. Dominique shivered.

Piece by piece their clothing found its way to the floor or on the table or chair. Limbs entwined. Lips caressed hidden places. Miles Davis's trumpet wailed the seductive "Moon Dreams" in perfect harmony with Dominique's cry of welcome to Trevor's entry. He filled her and she had never realized how empty she'd been until that moment.

Chapter 18

Dominique glided through her days with a secret smile on her face. It was hard to stay away from Trevor all day when she knew he was only feet away, working right above her. At least she had her hot, wet memories of their nights together help her along. They'd agreed—albeit she reluctantly—to keep business and their personal lives separate.

She didn't see how or why it should make a difference but Trevor was clear: at First Impressions he was there to do a job. He never wanted his crew to ever believe that he would compromise the integrity of the company and the job by doing more than what was on the contract.

Business and pleasure, what a tasty combination. She wanted to hug herself she felt so good and the first chance she got she called Zoe. If she didn't talk to someone she was going to burst with joy.

"Aw, girl, I wish I could get down there for lunch, but Makai has a cold and his sister is cranky. But I can listen. Tell, tell."

"Live would have been so much more fun, but I'm willing to settle for a phone call," she said, trying to sound upset and failing miserably. She was simply too happy and wanted to share that with her best friend. She spilled it all, the ups and downs, the rough days and erotic nights, of learning about each other and all the things they had in common.

"Wow…Dom…I am speechless, girl. I can't believe that a man has snatched my girl's heart. You know I have to meet him."

"You will. I'll figure something out."

"So, uh, you really don't have an issue with him being a man that works with his hands for a living? Because I know you, Dom, you have some real unique ideas about what a man is supposed to bring to your table."

"I know. I thought so, too. If I said I was totally over it, I would be lying. But I'm getting there. The more time I spend with Trevor the more it ceases to be important." She sat back in her office chair and spun it slowly from side to side. "Besides, he has great taste, his own sense of style, a kick-ass house…and those lips and…"

"TMI, TMI, too much information," Zoe squealed, cutting her off.

"Oh, but I can listen to you get all syrupy sweet and sticky about Jackson." She sang his name.

They both laughed.

"Okay. You got me on that one. I only want you to be sure."

"I am."

"It's always risky when you mix business and pleasure. Especially when one of them is cutting the pay check."

"It's going to be fine. And in another month or so, business won't be an issue."

"True. Well, you know I'm happy if you're happy."

"Thanks, sweetie. As soon as this project is over I'll plan a little party and you can meet Trevor then."

"Looking forward. Gotta run. The kids are waking up from their nap. Hugs."

Dominique hung up the phone. For a moment she leaned her head against the high back of the chair and closed her eyes. Zoe was always talking about her kids and her husband. The twins were absolutely gorgeous and smart and funny and she knew that they filled Zoe's life like nothing else could. She always said that Makai and Mikayla were truly a manifestation of the crazy, unexplainable love that she and Jackson shared.

Kids had been the furthest thing from Dominique's mind. They were nice and all, but it was even nicer to be able to give them back to their rightful owners. She smiled wistfully. What would it be like to have a child, to create a life with someone that you loved, to feel that love bloom inside of you?

Absently she pressed her hand to her stomach. *A*

child with Trevor. Her eyes slowly opened. That was a long way off. There was still a lot that she didn't know about Trevor, like why he harbored such distaste for "the other side of the tracks." Something happened in his life but he wouldn't talk about it. It had enough of an impact to color how he lived and what he thought. There was a part of him that he kept closed. And he had yet to show her what was stashed in the garage.

She blew out a breath. Enough daydreaming. She still had a business to run. She turned on her computer and checked her Outlook calendar. She had an appointment to meet with the Apple sales representative later in the day to finalize the details of her purchases for the school.

Day by day she came closer to seeing the fulfillment of her dream that had begun as a tiny seed. It still amazed her, at times, how her life and taken a complete one-eighty degree turn. A few years ago she was footloose and fancy-free, spending ridiculous amounts of money, partying, shopping and having what she thought was a good time.

She'd maxed out her credit card one time too many and it was her sister Lee Ann that finally shook some sense into her. Lee Ann was always the sensible one, the eldest daughter, a married woman. Dominique didn't want to hear it but the truth was, all the running around and playing dress-up was getting old. All of her friends had "something," a career, a passion, a real relationship. When Zoe got married, her empty reality began to sink in.

So she sat down one afternoon and had a heart-to-heart talk with her big sister. Dominique had never had to work hard for anything in her life. She finished school kicking and screaming and didn't have a clue what she wanted to do with her life. The only thing she knew anything about was clothes, shopping and fashion trends.

After tossing out the idea for a boutique, First Impressions was born. And the more she helped other women get their life on track and feel good about themselves, the better she felt. Having the GED program and resource center would be the culmination of everything. The positive impact that it would have on so many women was priceless. And, best of all, it felt good.

Every time she checked on the renovations she was blown away to see the progress that was made. The walls were all up. All new flooring ran throughout and pocket doors divided the spaces.

The carpenters had been working for the past week installing the cabinets, workstations and bookshelves. In the room that she'd set aside for the library they were building bookcases that expanded across two walls.

The top floor was being set up for a lounge and study area with a small but fully functional kitchen. The plumbing was done and the new windows were being installed. The balance of the work was cosmetic: painting, plastering and sanding the floors.

Earlier in the process she and Trevor would meet at the end of the day to go over the punch list and what the plans were for the following day. The meetings took place in Dominique's office. However, when their relationship shifted gears it quickly became clear that was a bad idea.

They'd almost been caught by Phyllis with their hands down each other's clothing. Fortunately, Dominique had a firm knock-first policy. Unfortunately, that almost mishap only reaffirmed Trevor's philosophy of separating their business and private lives.

Since then they would meet upstairs and Dominique would get a tour of the progress.

It was the part of the day that she looked forward to the most—that and the hours after dark.

Most nights she spent at Trevor's place. She even had her own drawer and shelf space in the bathroom.

Five months ago you could not have hypnotized her into believing where she would be in her life now. Trevor changed all that. He somehow rewired her thinking process. He made her believe that real love was a genuine thing, not just stories in a romance magazine and on soap operas. It was something real and tangible and it could be hers.

No, they hadn't crossed that great divide and spoken the about love or confessed it to each other. But she could feel it in his touch. She could see it in his eyes. It was only a matter of time.

Her desk phone rang, stirring her from her favorite pastime—daydreaming about Trevor.

She picked up the phone. "Hi, Phyllis."

"The new shipment of spring coats came in and there's a Jacqueline Lawson here to see you."

Dominique's neck jerked back from the phone. "Really? Okay. I'll be right out." She freshened her lipstick and went out front, wondering what in the world had brought her aunt to her doorstep.

"Aunt J. What are you doing here?" She walked up and kissed her cheek. "Phyllis, this is my aunt Jacquie, my dad's younger sister."

"Oh, we're fast friends, all ready," Phyllis said.

Dominique put her hand on her hip, "So, what brings you here?"

"I had some errands to run and I decided to come and see you since I don't see you at home anymore."

Dominique's face flushed with heat. Her eyes darted toward Phyllis, who was pretending that she was busy organizing scarves inside the glass counter. But Dominique could see the smirk on her face.

"Plus, I have some very interesting news to share with you." Her brows rose suggestively.

"What kind of news?"

"Let's talk about it over lunch?"

"I wish I could, Aunt J, but I have a meeting in about forty minutes."

"That's plenty of time for us to grab something to drink and chat."

Dominique gave a slight shrug. She turned to Phyllis. "If the Apple rep gets here before me just have him wait in my office."

"No problem."

"Is Joy coming in today?"

"At two. She has class this morning."

"Great. I'd like you to sit in on the meeting. Joy can cover the front."

The surprise on Phyllis's face was worth a snapshot. "Um, sure."

Dominique grinned. "We'll talk later."

The door bells chimed as Jacqueline and Dominique left. Dominique hooked her arm through her aunt's. "So, what's up?"

"Since I've had some time on my hands before I leave for Afghanistan, I decided to do a little research."

"Research? About what?"

"Let's stop in here." Jacqueline pointed to a little coffee shop on the opposite side of the street.

They were shown seats at a booth. Jacquie ordered a mocha latte and Dominique an iced tea.

"So, enough with the cloak and dagger. What is going on?"

The waitress placed the beverages on the table. "Can I get you ladies anything else?" She looked from one to the other.

"No, thanks," Dominique answered for both of them. She reached for her glass. An uneasy feeling settled in the pit of her stomach. "Okay, this is the part of the movie where the clever detective explains how the crime was committed." She took another sip.

"How much research did you do on T. Jackson Contracting?"

The muscles in her stomach clenched. "Why?"

"Did you look beyond the surface at all?"

"Aunt J, what are you talking about?"

Jacqueline's expression telegraphed bad news and Dominique wasn't sure she wanted to hear it. Jacqueline unzipped her tote bag and pulled out an envelope.

Dominique's throat went dry as dozens of scenarios raced through her head.

Jacqueline opened the envelope and took out photocopies of newspaper and magazine articles and web searches. They were all about Trevor. One article told about his ongoing philanthropic work restoring the 9th Ward of New Orleans—all pro bono. *Pro bono? How could he afford to do that?* There was even a picture of him with Brad Pitt and Angelina Jolie in front of a tract of new housing. And all of the articles touted Trevor Jackson as the owner of the most successful, independently owned construction company in the state of Louisiana. In other words, he was very wealthy, a wealth that was only estimated because the company was a private business. Apparently, throughout the years, Trevor had refused to give interviews and the photos that accompanied the articles looked like stock photos from a college yearbook, with the exception of the one in front of the housing being constructed. Yet, even there, an observer could tell that he didn't want to be photographed as he stood off to the side of the two superstars.

It didn't make sense. Why would he keep something like this from her? And more important, why did he "pretend" that money and the people who had it were dirty. He was one of the very people that he claimed not to respect.

If this was the worst of it, well he'd explain and they'd move on. But when she looked at her aunt, she knew that it wasn't.

Jacqueline stuck her hand in the envelope and pulled

out about a dozen photographs. She slid them across the table to her niece.

"I liked him from the moment we met," Jacqueline began as she watched Dominique's face flinch with each photo. "But I told him if he hurt you, he would regret it. I was driving through New Orleans about a week ago to do some shooting for an article. That's when I saw them."

Dominique's hands shook as she stared at images of Trevor and Vallyn. Vallyn's hand was on his, then caressing his cheek. They were seated together at a restaurant, standing together on a street corner holding hands. And even more disturbing was a photo of a young girl who looked up at Trevor with utter adoration.

Chapter 19

It was just about quitting time. Trevor's cell phone chirped. He had a text message. *Another one from Vallyn.* He blew out a breath of annoyance. She'd begun calling him two and three times a day on his company cell phone. Thankfully, she didn't have the number to his personal one.

I need to see you.

He shook his head. Since she'd turned back up in Baton Rouge and shown up at his office, she'd become a thorn in his side. If Traci was his daughter then he would do whatever he needed to do to make sure that she was taken care of. But what Vallyn was talking was pure craziness. And he wasn't agreeing to anything until she had a DNA test done on Traci.

He'd already been tested. All that was needed now was Traci's results. Max kept insisting that it was some kind of scam on Vallyn's part. Trevor tended to believe him, but to what lengths? Vallyn didn't need him to help her do anything. And if it was an issue of having a father for Traci—why now? Why seek him out five years after the fact? None of it made sense and until Vallyn did what he asked, he was staying as far away from her as possible.

The thought of her coming back after all this time and ruining the first solid relationship he'd had in years set his teeth on edge.

He hadn't wanted to get involved with Dominique. To him, she was a dressed-up version of Vallyn Williams, who flaunted her name and her money around and used everyone that wasn't nailed down. He'd been stupid enough to believe that *he* was different, that he'd gotten beyond her faux exterior to the real woman beneath. There was no real woman beneath. By the time he got slapped in the face with it, he was in too deep and the wake-up call changed his life.

Then Dominique dropped into his life like a shooting star. Hot to the touch, too bright and magnificent to stare at too long, but you couldn't let it go or turn away. He was hooked. As much as he tried to fight it, he couldn't. When they were together it was pure magic.

He'd begun to look forward to waking up with her in the morning, spending evenings with her, seeing her walking around his place as if she'd been doing it forever. And there were days when he really believed that he was able to love again.

Now all of that was threatened. He should have told Dominique what was going on from the beginning—

from the night he'd seen Vallyn at the Chateau. He'd acted like he didn't know her when Dominique went on to tell him who she was. He knew all too well. If not then, at least when the calls started. He hadn't. And now he wasn't sure where to begin.

He looked at the text message again and deleted it. It was nearly five-thirty. Dominique would have usually come up by now. He frowned. Maybe she had some clients downstairs.

He gathered up his things. Checked to make sure that the electricity and lights were turned off and that the windows that had not been replaced were sealed. They were expecting a big storm. The last thing they needed was to have major water damage from a window being left open. He did a final walk-through and locked up.

Trevor went out the back door then walked around to the front entrance. He didn't want to track all through the showroom with his work boots.

The door bell chimed.

"Hey, Phyllis. Is Dominique around?"

She gave him a hard look. Her lips barely moved when she spoke. "She's gone."

Why was he feeling a chill coming off Phyllis? "For the day?"

"I would assume so." She turned her back on him and hung some bracelets on the jewelry bar.

What the... "Thanks," he muttered. He walked out and took his cell phone from his pocket. He punched in Dominique's number. The phone rang five times and went to voice mail. He left a message asking her to call him. Then he sent her a text. Maybe she was planning on surprising him at the house. That brought a smile to his face.

He got in his truck and pulled off. When he walked into his house, Dominique wasn't there and neither were her things.

Between tears and fury Dominique struggled to keep her focus on the road. How could he not tell her? How did he think he could pull something like this off? She'd been a fool. Taken in by good looks, charisma and great sex. And she'd let those things blind her to the man Trevor really was—a liar.

After leaving her aunt she went blindly through her meeting and was thankful that Phyllis was in attendance since she had no idea what had taken place. Immediately after the meeting Phyllis walked the rep out and returned to Dominique's office. She'd shut the door behind her and insisted on knowing what was wrong. She'd said that Dominique had been like a ghost throughout the entire meeting and that wasn't like her.

Dominique tried to claim that it was nothing, just a lot on her mind, but before she could get all the words out she broke down and cried.

Between her sobs she spilled out Trevor's real background, which wasn't as awful as it was troubling. But the bombshell was the photographs with Vallyn Williams and the little girl.

"Did you ask him about it?"

Dominique shook her head. "He lied to me. What makes you think he won't lie again? I wouldn't know what to believe."

"There could be a perfectly good explanation."

She'd pushed back from her desk and stood. She took her purse from her desk drawer. "Whatever it is, I'm not in the mood to hear it." She started for the door.

"Where are you going?"

"I don't know," She pushed out a breath. "You can handle things here."

She'd gotten into her car and driven around for more than an hour before finding herself in front of Trevor's place. For all the joy she'd felt hours early, the weight of the ache in her heart had smashed it.

He'd given her a key, but she'd never used it until now. She'd let herself in, walked through the rooms and tried to see this "other" Trevor, the man he hid from her

The question that continued to plague her was that if he lied to her about who he really was, what he was about, then what other things were lies? How deep was his relationship with Vallyn? He clearly didn't want her to know that they knew each other. Why? And who was the little girl?

She thought about all of those things as she'd cleaned out her drawer, stuffed her belongings into a plastic bag and her toiletries in her purse. She took a final look around, lifted her chin, walked out and locked the door behind her.

That was hours ago. She didn't want to go home and face the questions of her aunt or see the concern in her face. So she found herself an hour away from home, pulling up in front of Zoe and Jackson's house. She shut off the car and walked along the path to the front door and rang the bell.

Moments later the door was pulled open. "Dom! What..." Zoe saw the look of anguish on her face and stopped mid-sentence. She reached out and took her hand and brought her inside.

The kitchen was warm and filled with the scents of rolls baking in the oven and a pot of stew on the stove top.

"I should have called," Dominique said.

"My door is always open. You don't need an invite." She passed her a cup of tea.

Dominique clasped the cup in both hands and slowly brought it to her lips.

Zoe waited. She knew her friend and she would tell her what was going on in her own time.

"Where's Jackson?"

"Still at the University. Tonight is his late night."

"The kids?"

"Thankfully, asleep." She smiled and then took a sip of her tea.

"Everything fell apart, Z." She blinked to keep the tears at bay. "I should have stuck to my plan of being a free spirit."

"Dom, what happened?"

Dominique covered her face with her hands and shook her head. Bit by bit she told Zoe about what her aunt had found out about the real Trevor Jackson and then the photographs.

Zoe was silent for a time, trying to process the information and wanting to be sure that she didn't jump to conclusions and say the wrong thing.

"Dom, one thing I've learned about relationships is that communication is key."

Dominique started to interrupt but Zoe held her off.

"I know what you are going to say. He didn't communicate with you. Now, I don't know what his reasons are. But neither do you and you won't if you don't talk to him."

Dominique pursed her lips. "But what about the pictures?"

Zoe raised a brow. "It could be anything."

"But why would he pretend that he didn't know her?"

"I can't answer that, Dom. The only one who can is Trevor. You need to talk to him. When you're ready."

Dominique stared into her cup of tea. She'd gone through a million scenarios in her head. None of them good. She looked at Zoe. "Suppose that's his daughter."

Zoe took a heavy breath. "If it is, you will have to decide how you want to handle it."

A rumble of thunder could be heard in the distance.

"Why don't you stay here tonight?"

"No." She shook her head. "I should start back before it gets bad out there."

"You're more than welcome, and the kids would be thrilled to see their auntie D in the morning."

"Sounds tempting. But maybe another time."

Another blast of thunder pummeled the night sky.

Dominique got up. "Kiss the kids for me."

Zoe put her arm around Dominique's shoulder. They walked out to the front door.

"Thanks," Dominique said.

Zoe wrapped her in a tight embrace and kissed her cheek. "Always here for you. And think about what I said, okay?"

Dominique nodded. "I will." She stepped out into the darkening evening and got into her car. Just as she pulled out of the driveway the first drops of rain began to fall.

Trevor was stretched out on his couch, listening to the thunder and watching the lightning illuminate the sky. He'd been calling Dominique off and on all evening. Every call went to her voice mail and she had yet to call him back.

He couldn't begin to imagine what had happened. Why was she upset? What he had done? He squeezed his eyes shut and threw his arm across his face. *He'd done plenty.* But Dominique didn't know anything about it. Or did she? But how?

His phone beeped. He sat up and snatched it from the table hoping that it was a text from Dominique.

He looked at the face on the phone. *Another text from Vallyn.* He tossed the phone back on the table then checked his personal cell to make sure that he hadn't missed a call or a message from Dominique. Nothing.

Rain pounded against the windows. He could hear the wind whistling through the trees and the water from the stream behind his house was churning as if it was being stirred with a whisk.

He got up from the couch and went to fix a drink. The next boom of thunder rattled the house. He heard a crash out back and went to look just as there was a pounding on his door that was muffled by the noise.

The lights flickered, dimmed and then everything went pitch black.

"Damn." He fumbled around in the kitchen drawer and located a flashlight. Luckily it worked. The generator should have kicked on already but it hadn't.

The banging started up again at the front door. This time he heard it. He pointed the flashlight in the direction of the front the house. He tried to see out of the window but it was too dark. He cracked the door open.

"Dom?" He jerked the door open and was whipped with wind and rain. He pulled her inside and slammed the door. She was soaked to the skin. "You need to get out of those clothes."

She pulled away from him and stood in the middle of the floor dripping wet. Her hair was plastered to her head and her clothes clung greedily to her every curve. She folded her arms.

Trevor stared at her in confusion. "You're just going to stand there dumping water all over the floor? You want to catch pneumonia?"

"The hell with your floor!"

"Dom…"

"Don't Dom me. You lied to me. You lied to me about who you are and you lied to me about knowing Vallyn Williams. I want to know why!"

Chapter 20

"It's not what you think."

"You don't know what I think! You have no idea what I think." She was breathing hard and pacing.

"I should have told you a lot of things from the beginning."

That stopped her in her tracks. She swiped water from her face and glared at him through the dimness. Her pulse raced. Maybe she didn't want to hear it. Maybe she could forget the whole thing and they could go on like nothing ever happened.

"I did know Vallyn."

A cold chill went through her. She hugged her arms around her body.

"We had a relationship a little over five years ago. I met her when I did a job for her father. We got involved." He turned and crossed the room. He placed the flashlight on the table and it shone like a single spotlight waiting for the headliner to step into the beam. "I believed that she really cared about me. I knew I cared about her and that we were going to make it work." He breathed heavily. "I came by one day to pick up some tools. She was in the den with a couple of her girlfriends. One of them asked her if she was tired yet of slumming with the help."

Dominique flinched.

"Vallyn said, 'he's good in bed and that's about it. We have nothing in common. He thinks that there can really be something between us. Imagine that.' They laughed."

Dominique's heart ached as she listened and heard the hurt in his voice. She could only imagine how he must have felt, how humiliated and betrayed. No wonder he threw up a wall between them when they first met. She swallowed over the knot in her throat.

"I haven't seen her in years, until recently. She came to tell me that we have a daughter."

Dominique felt sick.

"I asked her to have Traci…tested. She hasn't. I went to have my DNA testing done." He shrugged. "The rest is up to her." He looked over at Dominique, who had not moved.

"Is…is there a chance that…Traci is your daughter?"

He moved his head back and forth slowly. "I don't know, Dominique. She could be. But if resemblance has anything to do with it, she doesn't look anything like me."

She took a step. "What if she is your daughter?"

"If she is then I will do whatever I need to, to take care of her."

Dominique pressed her lips together. "That's what I hoped you would say," she said softly. She crossed the room and stood in front of him. "All I want is for you to be honest with me. That's all I ask. If we can talk and be honest with each other we can deal with anything, even this."

He took her hand. "I'm sorry. So sorry. I should have told you. I thought… I don't know what I thought. I guess I hoped it would simply go away."

"I know the Vallyn Williams type. She won't go away quietly. What I don't understand is why she waited all this time to tell you about Traci."

"I asked her the same thing."

"What did she say?"

"She said it wasn't important. She was here now."

Dominique shivered.

"You need to get out of those wet clothes."

Her teeth chattered.

He took the fleece throw that was on the couch and wrapped it tightly around her. She moved closer to him. He held her. She rested her head against his chest and the soothing beat of his heart flowed through her, warming her.

Trevor tilted up her chin with the tip of his finger and looked into the light of her eyes. "There's something else I haven't told you."

Her bottom lip trembled. "What?"

"I'm in love with you. Against all the defenses that I put up, you got through them."

She stroked his cheek. "Are you sure?"

"Very."

She touched her lips lightly to his. "Funny, I feel the same way."

"Say it," he murmured. "Tell me."

"I love you." And when she said the words, to a man, for the first time in her life, she felt her soul open and it was flooded with light and joy that brought tears to her eyes.

Trevor lowered his head and his mouth gently covered hers. He gathered her to him and tried to convey through his kiss the depth of his feelings for her.

Dominique sighed against his mouth. Her fingers pressed into his back. And she had no intention of letting him go, especially to the likes of Vallyn Williams.

"Let's go upstairs," he whispered.

"Let's…"

They gingerly picked their way around in the dark using the flashlight to guide them and made it upstairs, laughing and giggling like campers in the woods. Trevor didn't waste any time getting her out of her wet clothes. He wrapped her up in his robe and went to run a hot bath.

As quickly as he'd put the robe on her he took it off, picked her up in his arms and lowered her into the water. He peeled off his clothes and joined her.

"Now isn't this cozy," she hummed, taking a washcloth and dribbling the hot water over her shoulders.

"I can make it cozier."

"Is that right."

"Very."

He leaned forward and placed a tiny kiss on her neck, then the base of her throat and then trailed down to her breasts. Dominique squirmed in the water. He cupped her right breast in his palm and gently caressed while he administered to the other with his mouth. His free hand slipped down into the water and parted her thighs to find his hidden treasure waiting for him.

Dominique gasped when his finger slid inside of her and began to move in and out.

Steam from the water enveloped them. A flash of lightning lit up the sky.

Trevor lifted her up and she straddled him. He clasped the back of her head in his palm and covered her mouth with his as he pushed up inside her.

Dominique cried out from the shock and the sheer pleasure. She wrapped her arms around his neck and rode the wave.

They lay together thoroughly satisfied, entwined on Trevor's king-size bed, reveling in their new level of closeness and listening to the rain tap against the window.

Dominique lovingly caressed the expanse of his chest, explored the hard lines and feel of his skin beneath her fingertips.

"Since we are being totally honest with each other," she said softly. "I want to ask you something that I've been dying to know."

He twisted slightly so that he could look at her. "Sure. What is it?"

"What do you have in the garage?"

He burst into laughter. "Seriously," he sputtered.

"Yes, seriously," she said wide-eyed.

"Okay." He cleared his throat and schooled his expression. "A Porsche and a BMW convertible."

Dominique sat straight up in bed. "What?"

He offered a sheepish grin.

She stared at him for a long moment. "Next time we go out, we're going in the Porshe!"

"Deal." He pulled her into his arms and proceeded to pick right back up where they'd left off, just as the power came back on.

Chapter 21

If she had her way she would have stayed in bed all day curled up next to Trevor. But as she'd come to learn she couldn't always have what she wanted when she wanted it. And as Trevor reminded her during a quickie in the kitchen that morning, among the aroma of fresh brewed coffee and toasted bagels, they both had jobs to do and people were expecting them.

She tried to keep that at the forefront of her mind instead of thoughts of Vallyn Williams as she and Trevor left his home in separate cars and headed off to their respective offices. Even though Trevor had bared his soul to her last night, the unresolved issue of Vallyn was like the elephant in the room.

Why would she do something like that? It didn't make sense. Vallyn came from a well-to-do family. She certainly couldn't be doing it for the money. And the big question, why now?

She drove her car onto the street of her office building. The awning shone bright in the morning sunshine. She smiled. This was hers. It was something that she did on her own; without Daddy's help, without his money, without maxing out her credit cards. She'd had to learn to work with people from all walks of life, read contracts and hire staff and just plain old figure things out. It was scary at times, but seeing the faces of all the women that she helped was worth every ounce of fear.

And that's when the full and complete picture of Trevor materialized for her. He'd built a business from scratch, from hard labor. He'd made it successful by making good choices. And when he became successful, instead of touting the glory of it, he gave back to the neighborhood that made it possible for him to be where he is. He didn't want fanfare and notoriety. His net worth is not what mattered. What mattered was who he was as a man, as a human being. What he gave was invaluable—hope and a second chance.

Dominique smiled and her soul filled with wonder. That's what brought them together. Hope. That's what they saw in each other—the desire to help others change and improve their lives. Not with fanfare, but with dignity.

She wiped a stray tear of happiness from her eye and sniffed. *It was all about hope and second chances.* And had she not gone to his house last night and listened with her head and her heart, she may have never understood what was right in front of her all along.

Dominique drove around back where Trevor's truck

was usually parked, but today he had to go to his office first to meet with a potential client.

She got out and walked around to the front and stopped short when her aunt Jacqueline stepped out of her car that was parked at the curb.

"Aunt Jacquie…"

"Hi. Listen, I know I opened a Pandora's box yesterday."

Dominique looked down at her feet then at her aunt. "It's okay. Really. We talked. He told me everything, even about Vallyn. At least, all the everything that he knew."

Jacqueline bobbed her head. "Good, I'm glad. I knew I liked him. But, I would be a lousy journalist if I didn't follow up on a story."

"Meaning?"

"After I left you yesterday afternoon I went back to the house and did some more digging, which I should have done before I came to you…. Anyway, I think I know why Vallyn is really here…."

Trevor stood and extended his hand. "We look forward to working with you, Mr. Silver. Max and I will put together some figures and get back to you in about a week."

"I look forward to speaking with you. I've heard wonderful things about your company's work down in the 9th Ward over in Naw'lins" He bobbed his gray head. "It's a good thing that you're doing for all those families."

"Thank you, sir. It's a team effort."

"We'll talk next week." He extended his hand to Max. "Pleasure to meet you."

"You, as well."

"Nice suit," he said with a wink.

Max preened. "Thank you, sir."

When Mr. Silver had gone, Max turned to Trevor. "See a man with taste."

Trevor chuckled. "Whatever you say, man." His cell phone beeped. He took the phone from his pocket. It was a message from Dominique. Need 2 see u right away. Important.

"Everything cool?" Max asked.

"Yeah, yeah." He shoved the phone back into his pocket. "I'm gonna head over to the site."

"I'll ride over, too. I want to see how things are coming along."

"Cool. Let's go."

"I'll take my car."

For the entire twenty-five minute drive, Trevor ran through a million scenarios about what could be so important. Nothing concrete came to mind. One thing he did know, he couldn't put off dealing with Vallyn once and for all. Having a possible paternity issue hanging over his head was beginning to get to him.

He drove past the front entrance of First Impressions and around back to park. Max followed.

"You can go on inside," Trevor said, hopping out of the truck. "I need to speak to Dominique for a minute."

Max gave him an all-knowing smirk. He patted Trevor on the shoulder. "Go right ahead. I'll just go on in the back door so I won't bother nobody," he said in a bad servant parody.

Trevor chuckled and pointed a finger at Max. "You got issues. See you in a few." He walked away shaking his head. When he came around to the front door two women were coming out with big smiles and shopping bags. *Two satisfied clients.* He stepped aside to let them pass then walked in, hoping that he would get a warmer reception from Phyllis.

Phyllis was in one of the aisles straightening out the clothing on the hangers.

"Good morning."

She stopped midway and peered around the rack. For a moment her expression froze and then slowly softened with a warm smile. "Good morning." She adjusted the jacket on the hanger and came toward him. "I think I owe you an apology."

"No. You don't. You care about Dominique and it shows."

"So do you. And it shows," she added with a wink. She angled her head over her shoulder. "She's in her office."

He leaned down and kissed her forehead. "Thanks." Trevor didn't have to knock. The door was partially opened. He stuck his head in. "Anybody home?"

"Hi. Come in."

When he did he was surprised to find Dominique's aunt Jacquie seated in the club chair.

"Hello. Good to see you again." He extended his hand toward Jacquie, which she shook.

"You, too."

Trevor threw a quick look in Dominique's direction

hoping to get a hint at what was going on. What other bombshell did her aunt toss?

"Trevor, my aunt is probably one of the most important photojournalists in the world. Her research and photographs...well, they've been everywhere. I'm saying all this to say that when she came to me with the information and the pictures I knew that it wasn't something random. I knew that because I know my aunt. It's not who she is."

"But," Jacqueline cut in, "I didn't dig far enough." She opened a folder that she'd been holding on her lap. She handed it to Trevor.

"What is this?"

"Just read it. It explains everything."

Trevor's eyes ran over the words, stopped, went back and read them again. He finally looked up with an expression of sadness, anger and disbelief in his eyes. "Are you sure this is true?"

"Very," Jacqueline said.

"So, this whole thing was a setup?"

"She's broke. Her father cut her off and won't have anything to do with her. She became an embarrassment to her mother with her numerous affairs...several with married men."

Trevor drew in a shuddering breath. "I... It's so damned hard to believe. But I don't doubt that it's true."

"She knows that the child is not yours. The little girl is not five, which would make her the right age, she's four."

His chest heaved with relief.

She opened another folder and handed him a copy of Traci's birth certificate.

"How did you—"

Jacqueline half smiled. "Don't ask."

He looked at the birth certificate and Jacqueline was right. According to the date, there was no way that he could be Traci's father. He was long out of the picture. He scrolled farther down. In the box where the father's name would go it read: unknown.

"The real victim in all this is that little girl," Trevor said. "No way does she deserve this or a mother like Vallyn." He pushed up from his seat and faced Jacqueline. "Thank you." He turned toward the door with the folders in his hand.

"Where are you going?" Dominique asked.

"To take care of this once and for all."

Dominique clasped his upper arm. "I love you," she mouthed.

"I love you, too."

He got in his truck and scrolled through his messages until he found the one from Vallyn with her number. She was staying at some address across town. He had no intention of meeting her anyplace where he could be compromised. He called her and she picked up on the first ring.

"It's Trevor."

"Trevor, I was hoping you would call."

"I want to meet."

"Of course. You can come here."

"No. I don't think so. Do you know where Bottoms Up is?"

"I can find it. I'll need about an hour."

"Fine. I'll be there waiting."

* * *

Trevor arrived at Bottoms Up to the early lunch crowd. There were still plenty of tables available and he asked to be seated in the back. He ordered a burger and fries. He'd gone over what he wanted to say to Vallyn at least a dozen times. He knew it was best that they meet in a public place because there was no telling what he might have done or said behind closed doors.

His waitress arrived with his lunch and he realized he was really hungry. He was halfway through his burger just as Vallyn appeared in the door way. He watched her look around for him before he stood up. She spotted him and pointed him out to the hostess who led her to the table.

He didn't bother to help her with her seat.

She glanced around. "Do you come here often?" she asked with that tone that he'd grown to hate over time. One that reeked of "I'm better than you."

"Actually, yes, when I'm *slumming.*" He watched her flinch.

She placed her purse on the table. "Is it going to be that kind of conversation? I thought you came here to talk to me about financial arrangements for Traci."

"Actually, I did." He pushed the folder across the table at her.

"What is that?"

"Open it and you tell me."

Her nostrils flared. She ran her tongue across her lips and flipped the folder open.

Trevor took a great deal of pleasure in watching her haughty expression begin to crumble, her throat worked up and down and her eyelids fluttered in disbelief.

"Where did you get this?" she asked, her voice almost ghostlike.

"It doesn't matter. What matters is that you were going to use that little girl to benefit yourself. And use me to make it happen. What kind of woman are you?"

"You…you don't understand."

"Understand what, Vallyn? How to be a decent human being?"

"I have nothing." Her eyes widened with what looked like fear. "I can't go home. My father cut me off. My mother won't have anything to do with me…."

"Where is Traci's father?"

She glanced away. "I…I don't know."

"What about all of those 'friends' of yours. Why can't they help you?"

"They were never my friends. Not really. They were around because of what I had, who I was. My family name that could open doors for them." She sniffed back her tears. "I know you won't believe this but…you were the only person in my life that didn't care about all of that."

"You're right, I don't." He tossed his napkin on top of his plate. "We're done, Vallyn. Done."

"I loved you, Trevor." She grabbed his hand. "And I was stupid to choose that other life over you."

He stood and looked down at her upturned face. "We live and we learn." He pulled his hand away and walked out.

Chapter 22

The final touches for the grand opening of First Impressions' Second Chance Learning Center were almost complete. The caterers were bringing in the last of the hors d'oeuvres and the small combo that she'd hired was setting up. The guests weren't scheduled to arrive for another hour and she was a nervous wreck. It was as if she'd never hosted a party in her life.

When she looked around she was still awestruck at the transformation the two floors had taken from dark, dangerous, dank rooms to bright, safe, totally stylish spaces equipped with top-of-the-line computers, gleaming hardwood floors, shelves of books and training materials, audio and video equipment, which was Trevor's idea, and a full kitchen and lounge. It was all hers. She'd actually done it. And the number of women's lives she would be able to change was immeasurable.

She'd spent the prior two weeks screening potential instructions and going over applications for women who'd applied to the classes. Many of them had been referred by the local shelters and then word of mouth from the many women who'd used First Impressions' clothing services. As it stood now, she had a waiting list before the doors even officially opened.

"How's the lady of the evening doing?" Trevor asked, sneaking up behind her and kissing the back of her neck.

She turned into his arms. "Better now." She smiled up at him. Although she would never be able to get Trevor in a suit and tie on a regular basis, when he did get dressed he "put it on," as her younger brother, Justin, would say. Her man was board-of-health clean and he just smelled so good. She kissed his lips then brushed them lightly with the pad of her thumb to remove the lipstick.

"You look great."

"You look edible and I'm going to prove it to you later." He winked.

"Can't wait," she whispered. "No, no…put that tray on the table on the end," she instructed one of the delivery men.

He kissed the top of her head. "It's going to be fine. See you in a bit."

And he was right. The grand opening was a stellar success and her aunt, always the journalist, had arranged for news coverage. Both her sisters and their husbands had come down to help her celebrate, and Zoe and Jackson were there with the kids. Rafe was charming the ladies, of course, and Justin actually brought a date. But she could not have been more stunned when she looked into the milling crowd and saw her father.

Several reporters were trying to get an interview and he politely declined as did her junior senator brother-in-law Preston.

Dominique made her way through the crowd until she was in front of him. No matter how old she became or what she'd done or accomplished, being in her father's presence always made her feel like a little girl.

"Daddy...I had no idea you were coming."

"I wanted to see what all the fuss was about. Looks like you have yourself a pretty fancy place."

She laughed nervously. "Not too fancy." She slid her arm through his and looked up at him. "I'm really glad you're here."

He patted her hand. "Where can an old man get a drink around here?"

"Come with me, Daddy," Lee Ann said, "Dom has guests to entertain." Lee Ann whisked her father away and Phyllis took her place.

"It's probably about time for you to say a few words and your aunt said a reporter wants to speak with you before the evening is over."

Dominique nodded. She walked over to where the combo was playing and asked the leader if she could borrow the microphone.

"Good evening, everyone."

By degrees the room quieted and all eyes turned in Dominique's direction.

"Thank you all for coming and supporting this important endeavor. When I started First Impressions, I simply thought I would be able to give really nice clothes to women who needed it. But as I got to know those wonderful women who come through the doors, it's more than the clothes, it's about feeling worthy. It's about knowing that there are others out there who want you to succeed. And it's about second chances." Her gaze sought out her father and her aunt.

A murmur of agreement bounced around the room.

"And so is the Second Chance Learning Center. It is a place for women to have the opportunity to 'try it again.' To give themselves the opportunity that they missed or could not fulfill for a variety of reasons, and hopefully change their lives in the process. We all make mistakes. We all fall short of our dreams sometimes. But with help and support we can have a second chance to make it right. I want to thank T. Jackson Contracting for the magnificent job in turning a disaster into a showplace. Apple Corporation for helping us secure ten computers and a tech to help train us. My family, my friends and my ladies who gave me a second chance to do a good thing. Thank you all and have a great evening." She handed back the microphone and was quickly surrounded by everyone who wanted to shake her hand.

The food was eaten and the wine was sipped and soon the evening wound down to an end.

Branford was talking with Preston and he excused himself to come to where Dominique sat, happy and tired.

"I'll going to be heading out. I have a flight back to D.C. in an hour."

She pushed up from her seat. "Your being here really means a lot to me."

"I'm really proud of you, Dominique. You have done an amazing job with your company, and I'm so very proud."

She felt her throat get tight and her eyes begin to tear. "Thank you."

He kissed her cheek. "You take care of yourself."

"I will. Daddy, wait, there's someone I want you to meet."

"If it's that young man of yours, Trevor, we've met. He introduced himself to me."

Her heart thundered.

"I told him how lucky he was and make sure he treats you like the princess you are." He squeezed her hand and walked out.

Dominique was sure she must be dreaming to hear those words come from her father. She would cherish them for as long as she lived.

More than an hour later, the rooms were empty save for Dominique and Trevor. They sat side by side on one of the couches in the lounge. He topped off her glass of champagne.

"Congrats, baby."

"Couldn't have done it without you."

"I know," he teased and touched his glass to hers.

She shoved him with her elbow. "So you met my father."

He nodded. "That I did. I can see where you get your passion from?"

"Passion?"

"Yeah, passion. In the short time that I spent talking with your father, I knew that he was a passionate man. Passionate about what he does for the country and passionate about his family. He rode you so hard all those years because he knew what you were capable of. And he was right." He leaned over and kissed her forehead.

She ducked her head then rested it on Trevor's shoulder.

"You know what else I discovered?" he said against her ear.

"What?"

He slipped one skinny strap from her shoulder and then the other. "That mixing business with pleasure isn't so risky, after all."

She twisted around so that she could look into his eyes. "I was thinking the very same thing."

Slowly he lowered his head until his lips touched hers. She sighed softly against his mouth. And when he held her and whispered over and over how much he loved her, she fully understood that when love comes it may not always be who you expected or how you expected it to arrive, but you'll know it when you feel it. She felt it deep down in her soul—where she carried it for Trevor and where she would nurture her love for him for the rest of her days.

Epilogue

Vallyn opened her purse and plucked out her last twenty-dollar bill. Her stomach knotted. She glanced over her shoulder and watched her daughter sleep. Pain hitched in her throat. She pressed her fist to her mouth to hold back the sob.

She'd been so stupid and selfish and greedy. She'd lost everything and she didn't have a clue what to do next. How was she going to take care of her child?

There was a knock on her hotel door.

"Yes?"

"I have a package for Ms. Williams."

She pulled her robe tighter around her body and cracked the door open. A messenger stood there with an envelope and a clipboard in his hand.

"Ms. Williams?"

"Yes."

He turned the clipboard around. "Sign here, please."

She signed her name and took the envelope. "Thank you," she murmured before closing the door. She turned the envelope over. There was no address.

She stuck her nail under the flap and tore the top open. She pulled out a typed letter. Her hand shook. It was from Trevor.

Vallyn,

Whatever you are, whatever you have become, your daughter should not be a victim of your mistakes. I don't think I could live with myself knowing that an innocent child is suffering in any way. It's not the kind of man I am. I want to make sure that she has a chance in life, the one you almost deprived her of.

Dominique and I have set up a trust account in her name. The bank information is enclosed. It can't be touched by you—ever. Traci will have full access when she turns eighteen.

I hope you find a way to do the right thing for yourself and for Traci.

Trevor

She read the letter three times before re-folding it and putting it back in the envelope. Slowly she sat down on the side of the bed. She looked at her sleeping daughter.

Traci had a chance for a future, thanks to a man that she'd betrayed in the worst way.

She understood now more than ever why she'd loved

him. And had she not allowed the trappings of a life-style to dictate her happiness, they may have been to-gether now. But they weren't. She had no one to blame but herself. He was with a woman now who loved him for who he was. Something that she realized too late.

"I was thinking about us taking a little trip," Trevor was saying as he stirred the spaghetti sauce in the pot.

"A trip. Wow, babe, now isn't really a good time with the school just getting off the ground and—"

He put his finger to her lips. "We have time to plan for it."

She frowned. "What are you talking about?"

"I figure at least six months?"

"To plan a trip? You're kidding, right?"

He half shrugged. "Well, how long does it usually take to plan a honeymoon?"

"A…a honeymoon…what?"

He stuck his hand in his pocket and pulled out a daz-zling diamond ring. "Yes, the honeymoon we'll take after you say yes to being my soulmate in front of God and family." He took her hand and held it. "Marry me, Dom."

Her eyes glistened with tears of joy. "Only if you let me drive the Porsche!"

He swept her in his arms and he knew that whatever the future held Dominique Lawson would handle it with style!

* * * * *

We hope you enjoyed reading SULTRY NIGHTS
by Donna Hill, the third book in
THE LAWSONS OF LOUISIANA *series.*
If you missed reading the book that launched
this popular series,
SPEND MY LIFE WITH YOU,
we have included the first chapter for your review.

Chapter 1

Lee Ann Lawson leaned toward her dressing table mirror and fastened the diamond studs into her ears, just as the booming voice of her father called out to her from the other side of the Louisiana mansion.

"Coming!" she called back, tightening the belt of her white silk robe around her slim waist and wondering as she padded barefoot along the winding hallway what it was that he couldn't find. She smiled inwardly and prepared herself to fuss over her daddy for the next few minutes. She was stopped halfway when one of her twin sisters, Dominique, leaped out from her bedroom door, hands planted boldly on her round hips.

"Sis, would you please tell my darling dull twin that this dress does not show too much cleavage!" She flashed a scowling look at her mirror image, who sat demurely on a cushioned footstool.

Lee Ann looked Dominique up and down. Of the two, Dominique was always the flamboyant one, ready at the drop of a hat to be the center of attention. And her dress definitely did that. Cut in the front to nearly her navel, the sparkling silver floor-length gown barely held her size Cs in place.

"You sure your dolls aren't going to pop out and introduce themselves at the party?" Lee Ann asked, only half in jest.

Desiree covered her mouth and laughed. "Told you, Dom. And it's the same thing Mama would have said."

Dominique pouted. "I have a cover-up."

"Be sure you have it with you," she warned. She peeked around Dominique. "You look beautiful, Desi. And you, too, Dom," she said with a big-sister wink.

"Lee Ann!" Branford bellowed.

The sisters exchanged a knowing look as Lee Ann hurried down the hallway. The voices of her brothers, Rafe and Justin, floated to her from the main room below. She couldn't wait to see her handsome brothers all decked out. She tapped on her father's door.

"Come in."

She pushed the partially opened door and stepped inside. Even after five years, she still had not adjusted to the reality that every night her father slept alone and that their beloved mother was no longer with them. As the oldest girl, she'd stepped into the role of caregiver for her mother during her mother's long illness and then the caregiver for her family—her father in particular.

"Hey, Daddy. Sorry, I got waylaid by those girls." She laughed lightly and crossed the circular room to where her father sat on the edge of the king-size bed struggling with his cuff links. "Here, let me." Her slender honey-toned fingers moved expertly to insert the onyx cuff links and fasten them.

"You fix me up just like your mama, God rest her soul," he murmured and affectionately patted Lee Ann's hand.

The ache in his voice twisted inside of Lee Ann and settled where it always did—in the center of her heart. She leaned over and kissed her father's cheek then sat back and adjusted his tie, turning her head right then left as she did.

Her father was one of the most powerful men in the state of Louisiana. Senior Senator Branford Lawson not only carried clout but respect across both sides of the aisle. Some of his closest friends were those who for the average person were only seen on television and in newspapers, but to her they were Aunt Hillary or Uncle Bill. At any given time, the Lawson mansion would become the epicenter for political gatherings. She remembered one day as a young girl waking up and seeing former president Carter sitting in the kitchen sipping coffee with her father.

It had been her mother, Louisa, who'd overseen the Lawson household and clan like the queen of England oversaw her country. She was the consummate Southern hostess, the nurturing but watchful mother and loyal and devoted friend. Lee Ann became the woman she was because of her mother.

Lee Ann pushed back the memories as they threatened to overtake her. With her mother's passing, Lee

Ann stepped into her mother's role. It was a big responsibility, but she did it with love.

"Perfect," she announced of her handiwork. "Now stand up and let me take a good look."

Her father dutifully did as he was asked.

"Looking good, Daddy."

He leaned down and kissed her forehead. "That's what all the ladies say," he teased. Then he looked at her as if seeing her for the first time. He frowned. "Why aren't you dressed?"

Her right brow elevated. "That's what I was doing when I was summoned."

He pretended to miss her point. "Well, don't stand around," he said, flinging his hand in her direction to shoo her out. "Get yourself together. You know how I hate being late."

Lee Ann shook her head and grinned. "Yes, Daddy." She returned to her room, took her dress from the walk-in cedar closet and was wiggling into it when her brother Rafe came knocking.

"Now look at you," he hummed in that tone he reserved for when he wanted something.

Rafe leaned against the frame of her door, a glass of bourbon in one hand and his other hand tucked into the pocket of his tuxedo slacks, as smooth and sleek as a panther and just as deadly to the ladies. Raford James Lawson, the eldest of the Lawson clan, was a notorious playboy not only in the United States but abroad, as well, although he swore, with a wink and a smile, that those rumors weren't true. At thirty-six, he was unattached, wealthy, handsome, smart and came

from a powerhouse family. He'd been profiled countless times in major magazines as one of the country's
most eligible bachelors, sexiest man and heir apparent
to his father's Senate seat. Rafe would agree to the first
two, but the last stood as a bone of contention between
father and son. He'd rather spend his days traveling,
loving women and playing his sax. Politics weren't in
his blood. But his father wouldn't hear of it.

Lee Ann pursed her cherry-tinted lips and ran her
hazel eyes along the long lines of her big brother. "A
little early for bourbon, don't you think?"

"Never too early for bourbon, cher," he teased, rais-
ing his glass to her in salute before taking a sip.

"At least make yourself useful. Come zip me." She
turned her back to him and waited for his real reason
for descending upon her.

"Listen, sis…"

Here it comes, she thought. "Yes, sugah, what is it?"
She turned around to face him, looked up into his bottomless black eyes, framed by silky lashes, and knew
without question what women saw in her brother. And
no matter how much warning they were given they kept
coming.

"About tonight…"

"Yes?" She buttoned the top button of his shirt then
began fashioning his bow tie.

"I know Daddy wants to show me around like some
prized pony and have me glad handing all night, but
there's this new blues club down in the Quarter. If I can
get there before midnight, I can get in on the last set."

His smooth face and midnight eyes literally danced

with excitement and matched the almost childlike urgency of his voice.

"Rafe," she cautioned. "You know how Daddy feels about that."

"I know, baby sis. That's why I need your help…to distract him while I get out of there," he cajoled. He leaned down to her ear. "Please."

Lee Ann playfully pushed him away. "Don't start your foolishness with me, Rafe Lawson. I'm not one of your starry-eyed ladies."

He chuckled. "You wound me, cher."

She put her hands on her hips and then wagged a warning finger at him. "I'll do this for you…again. But I'm warning you, Raford. You get yourself in any trouble tonight and you're on your own. Understood?"

"Yes, ma'am." He leaned down and put a sloppy wet kiss on her cheek.

"Aggg. You know I hate when you do that! Ruining my makeup. Get on out of here."

Raford laughed on his way to the door. "Love you, too," he called out.

Lee Ann shook her head in affectionate amusement, walked over to her dressing table mirror to inspect the damage then touched up her makeup.

"Lee Ann."

She turned. Her younger brother, Justin, had his head sticking in her door, the spitting image of their mother with his sandy-brown complexion, tight curly hair and to-die-for dimples. Although he was still growing into his looks, Justin was one handsome young man.

"Daddy said if you aren't down in two minutes we're

leaving without you. I'm to make sure you get downstairs," he said with a twinkle in his eyes. They both
knew that Branford Lawson was more bark than bite,
and the last person he'd get on the wrong side of was
Lee Ann.

"Coming. Don't you look handsome?" She crossed
the room and stood in front of him. Lee Ann was the
only one who could make Justin blush. He, like his
brother, towered over their petite sisters, and Justin, at
twenty-three, beat his brother out by an inch of Rafe's
six-foot-three-inch height. By habit, she straightened his
tie and smoothed her hands over his broad shoulders.
"Let me get my purse and I'm ready."

The family filed into the waiting limo, and it sped
off into the balmy Louisiana night.

By the time they arrived at the estate of Congressman Jeremiah Davis, the reception portion of the evening was getting underway. Waiters glided between
the bejeweled guests with platters of mouthwatering
appetizers and flutes of champagne. The thousand-
dollar-per-plate affair was a fundraising event for the
incumbent congressman. And with the downward
spiral of the economy on the watch of the Democrats,
he needed all the support he could get.

Jeremiah and Branford had been friends since
they were in knee-highs and had followed each other
throughout their school years, served as each other's
best man at their weddings and were godfathers to
their children. There was a bond between them that

was stronger than most brothers, and the Lawson clan adored their uncle Jerry.

"It's about time you all got yourselves here," Jeremiah said, kissing cheeks and shaking hands.

Jeremiah could only be described as round. Everything about him was round, from the top of his head down to his bowlegs. He often reminded Lee Ann of one of those children's toys that rocked back and forth and rolled around without ever falling over.

"Hi, Uncle Jerry," Lee Ann said, becoming enveloped in his hearty embrace. He held her back at arm's length and looked her over.

"Looking more like your beautiful mama with every passing day," he said softly.

Lee Ann smiled. What could she say? She'd run out of words from the often heard comment. A part of her felt so complimented to be compared to her mother, then there was another part that felt overwhelmed by the comparison that she felt she could never live up to.

Her sisters and brothers had already dispersed into the crowd. They'd been trained well, since they were old enough to be introduced to the world. They knew how to work a crowd, gain information without giving any, befriend newcomers and leave an indelible impression on everyone that they met. They were the epitome of the political elite family, which was often as much of a burden as it was a badge of honor.

Lee Ann slipped her arm through Jeremiah's. "And where is Aunt Lynn? I don't see her."

"Probably worrying the waiters to death." He chuckled good-naturedly. "You know your aunt. Walk with me outside. I need some air already."

Lee Ann laughed lightly, and it stopped as if a cork had slid down her throat. A warm wave fluttered in her stomach as they drew closer to the group assembled near the balcony.

She'd only seen him from a distance in the past, although she'd watched him closely during his run for the junior senate seat and listened to her father extol his virtues. Although Lee Ann worked closely with her father as his personal consultant, she tended to steer clear of the interactions of the power brokers, rarely visited Washington and worked out of the family home or occasionally at her father's local office in Baton Rouge.

"Congressman," one of the ladies announced. All eyes turned in their direction.

Jeremiah let out a hearty laugh. "Now that's the way I like to make an entrance, introduced by a beautiful woman." The group dutifully chuckled. He turned to Lee Ann. "I'm sure most of you know Lee Ann Lawson, the real power behind the senator."

Lee Ann's face heated. She looked from one to the other. "He gives me too much credit."

"All deserved, my dear." He slipped her arm out from his and patted her hand. "Senator Preston Graham, have you met Lee Ann?"

"I'm sure if I did I would have remembered," he responded, his dark eyes doing a slow stroll across her face. He extended his hand toward her.

Lee Ann stretched out her hand, and he leaned down and kissed the top of it. "My pleasure." A smile teased the corners of his mouth. "I feel as if I already know you."

She tilted her head slightly to the side. "Why is that?"

"Your father talks about you all the time."

Her gaze darted away for an instant. "He does the same about you."

"Is that right? Hope it's all good." Light danced in his eyes.

"Yes, it is. He thinks very highly of you. And congratulations, by the way, on your win."

"I'm still getting my feet wet. Your father is an excellent mentor."

"That he is."

"Can I get you a drink?"

"Yes. Thank you."

After they both realized that he was still holding her hand, Preston chuckled. "Maybe it's a sign that we should go out together."

Lee Ann's soft laugh brushed against him like a caress. He tucked her hand in the curve of his arm.

"I'm surprised we haven't officially met before," Preston said as they crossed the expansive room.

"I try to stay behind the scenes except when my father needs me front and center." She smiled and tried to keep her feet moving one in front of the other even as the electric energy of Preston Graham bounced off her, short-circuiting her brain.

"You do a very good job of it, considering that you are his political adviser of sorts. At least that's my understanding."

"I do oversee his activities, but it's more like a personal assistant," she said.

They reached the bar. "What will you have?"

"A white wine spritzer."

He gave the order to the bartender and ordered a bourbon for himself.

"My brother's favorite drink," she commented as they were served.

"A man after my own heart," he joked. "And apparently the ladies, as well," he added with a lift of his chin in the direction of her brother.

Rafe was in a close conversation across the room with a stunning woman who Lee Ann hadn't recalled seeing before.

She shook her head in amusement. "Rafe does keep busy."

"And what about you? When you're not personally assisting your father, what do you do?"

She was thoughtful for a moment. "Running the house and keeping an eye on my sisters and brothers is pretty much a full-time job."

"It doesn't sound as if you allow time for yourself." He stared into her eyes over the rim of his tumbler.

Her heart fluttered. "I find ways to enjoy myself," she said in her defense.

Preston studied her for a moment and decided to let the topic go. "What's it like growing up with a father like Branford?"

They walked together to an available table and sat down.

Lee Ann's smile was wistful. "Where can I begin?"

She gazed around the room. "My life has been pretty much like this for as long as I can remember," she said with a sweep of her hand. "Politics and parties and entertaining and being in the spotlight has been a way of life."

He heard something in her voice, a note of hesitancy, regret. He couldn't be sure.

"I would think it was pretty exciting." He sipped his drink and watched the muted light play across her finely etched features.

Her warm hazel eyes flickered across his face. "I suppose it would be looking in from the outside. But to us, all of the people who everyone else reads about were like family." She drew in a breath, reached for her glass and realized that her hand was shaking. She concentrated on bringing the glass to her lips without spilling her drink. "What about you?" she asked, steering the conversation away from herself, a topic that she didn't relish discussing.

Preston set his glass down, tilted his head slightly to the side, his full lips pressed lightly together and puckered out. "Well, I'm a product of a single teenage mom. Public schooling. My mama worked two jobs that added up to one most of my life." His dark eyes drifted away from Lee Ann. "She would tell me every day that she expected me to make something of myself. She wasn't working so I could grow up to be a nobody." The corner of his mouth jerked as the images of those days of "have not" flashed through his head. "As soon as I was old enough, I got a part-time job after school, packing groceries, delivering whatever needed to be delivered, flipping burgers, waiting tables. You name it, I did it at one point or the other."

"It must have been hard."

He looked directly at her. "I suppose to someone looking in from the outside," he said, playing with her statement to him. "But like you, it was the only life I knew. Sometimes I would see the other kids in their new sneakers or tooling around town in their daddy's car, walking into fancy houses." His face and voice took on a hard edge like a tide that suddenly rushed to shore pulling the sand out from under your feet—unexpected and scary. "I knew there was more out there than what was in front of me, and I had to find a way to get it. My life and my mama's struggling made me what I am. Determined and focused to get what I wanted. And I did, but I'm not finished yet."

Lee Ann held her breath, anticipating what, she wasn't sure. And then he smiled and the tide slowly receded, and she was standing on solid ground again.

"Don't mind me, I can get a little caught up in my own rhetoric sometimes," he said, catching the look of apprehension in her eyes. "Come dance with me." He stood and extended his hand, once again the dashing, gallant gentleman.

Lee Ann placed her hand in his, and he helped her to her feet. They moved onto the dance floor, and then she was in his embrace. And he was all around her, his arms, the lines of his body, his scent. Her head barely reached his shoulders, so she found herself resting it against his broad chest as they moved in harmony, swaying easy to the music of the band, and she had the oddest sensation that she had done this all before, with this man. It was all so familiar and right. But, of course, that couldn't be true. She'd never met him before.

Preston didn't want to give in to the urgent need to pull her closer, to feel her fully against him. The sensation of her being so close and still so far was messing with his head. The fresh scent of her hair, the barely there fragrance that she wore combined with the heat of her body had him coiled tight as a rattlesnake. He had to concentrate on the music, the aroma of food, the smatterings of conversation that floated around him to keep his mind off what she was doing to his body. In as much as he wanted her closer, there would be no doubt about her effect on him if he did. She'd be sure to think that he was some randy fool who couldn't control his urges. He was almost thankful when the music ended. He needed some air and some space.

He released his hold around her waist and stepped back. She tilted her head up to look at him; the dewy softness of her lips, the light dancing in her eyes and the tiny pulse beating in her throat had him wanting to forget what was proper and simply take her mouth and sample it until they couldn't take it anymore.

"Thank you for the dance," he managed to say, his voice thick and jagged. "I'm going to go mingle a little."

"Oh…of course." She put on a practiced smile and wondered what she'd done wrong.

He took her elbow and walked her back to the table. "Thanks again for the dance and the conversation."

She offered a tight smile while she watched him

walk away, and for reasons that she couldn't explain she felt like bursting into tears.

"Hey, baby doll, come on and dance with your big brother." Rafe curved his arm around her waist before turning her petite body into his.

His arms were strong, familiar and secure, and for a few minutes she could forget how small and insignificant she felt, which of course was ridiculous. It was just a conversation, a drink and a dance. No big deal.

"You're stiff as a board." He peered down at her. "What's wrong? Did he say something out of the way to you?"

She heard the sudden rise in his tone. The smooth easy cadence was gone. Lee Ann dared to look up at his piercing dark eyes.

"Don't be silly," she soothed. "I'm fine, and no, he didn't say anything out of hand."

Rafe took a hard look over his shoulder, seeking out the young senator as if seeing him would somehow validate what his sister said. He turned back to Lee Ann. "You sure, because I have no problem sharing a few words with him man-to-man."

Lee Ann gently pressed her hands against Rafe's hard chest. "I can take care of myself. Thank you very much," she added with a slight smile.

He leaned down and kissed her forehead then skillfully moved with her around the floor. "All you have to do is say the word," he said, his protective instincts kicking into high gear. He'd always been that way with his sisters, since they were all little. He took great pride in being the big brother, and yes, it was true that he loved women but none more than his sisters and, of course, his mother. Lee Ann was the one most like their mother, and he was sure that was one of the reasons they were so close, as children and as adults. "I'll hang around if you need me to," he said.

"No, please. I know your lips are itching to play, so whenever you're ready just go on. It'll be fine. I'll tell Daddy something or nothing." She grinned at him.

The dance came to an end, and they walked across the grand ballroom out to the balcony. The air was still heavy and filled with the scent of a hot spring night. Beyond the cove of streets, the lights of the city peeped in and out, and the soft sound of the Mississippi rolled gently in the distance.

For a fleeting moment, caught in the beauty of the evening, Lee Ann wished that she was peering out into the night, whispering soft words and sharing light laughter with her own someone special.

"Looks like everyone who's anyone is here tonight," Rafe commented, taking a brief look over his shoulder into the main room.

"Well, you know Uncle Jerry never does anything halfway." She continued to stare out into the night.

Briefly Rafe put his hand around her shoulder, and she tilted her head to rest it against him. "Can I get you a drink, a plate of food?"

"Another spritzer would be nice, thanks."

"Be right back."

She inhaled deeply and reentered the ballroom, watched the milieu move around her and felt so apart from the activities. It was so unlike her, she thought, not to be like a butterfly flitting from one guest to the next, enjoining and cajoling as if she was the hostess. Smiling, as was her habit as she passed familiar faces, she found herself back on the balcony, sure that her brother would instinctively find her.

She leaned against the balustrade with her back to the Mississippi, and her stomach quivered when she saw Preston heading with purpose in her direction. She tried to glance away, ignore his approach, but it was too late.

He walked right up to her, cutting off everything and everyone around them. He took up her vision.

"I'm usually much more the Southern gentleman than I was earlier," he said. Thick lashes lowered over his dark eyes for an instant then settled on his face. A half-shy smile tickled the corners of his rich mouth. "I... You rattled me, Ms. Lawson," he said. The soft twangy cadence of his voice was both charming and unnerving.

Lee Ann tilted her head slightly to the right, for the first time since they met having a sense of standing on firm ground without her legs wobbling beneath her. She smiled and, always the tactful lady being Louisa Lawson's daughter, said, "Senator Graham, I have no idea what you mean."

The imaginary rift they'd created was crossed with their relieved laughter.

REQUEST YOUR FREE BOOKS!

2 FREE NOVELS
PLUS 2 FREE GIFTS!

KIMANI™
ROMANCE

Love's ultimate destination!

Harlequin® Desire

ALWAYS POWERFUL, PASSIONATE AND PROVOCATIVE.

**NEW YORK TIMES AND USA TODAY
BESTSELLING AUTHOR**

BRENDA JACKSON

**PRESENTS A BRAND-NEW
WESTMORELAND FAMILY NOVEL!**

FEELING THE HEAT

Their long-ago affair ended abruptly and
Dr. Micah Westmoreland knows Kalena Daniels
hasn't forgiven him. But now that they're working
side by side, he can't ignore the heat between them...
and this time he plans to make her his.

Also available as a 2-in-1 that includes
Night Heat.

Available in April wherever books are sold.